SUCCESS PRINCIPLES *of* Bill Gates

SHIKHA SHARMA

PRABHAT
PRAKASHAN

Published by
PRABHAT PRAKASHAN PVT. LTD.
4/19 Asaf Ali Road,
New Delhi-110002 (INDIA)
e-mail: prabhatbooks@gmail.com

ISBN 978-93-5562-733-9

SUCCESS PRINCIPLES OF BILL GATES
by *Shikha Sharma*

Edition
First, 2024

Price
₹ 300 (Rupees Three Hundred Only)

Printed at
Sanjay Printers, Sahibabad

Author's Note

Bill Gates, born on October 28, 1955, in Seattle, Washington, is widely regarded as one of the most influential figures in technology and entrepreneurship. Co-founder of Microsoft Corporation, Gates played a pivotal and key role in revolutionizing the personal computer industry and shaping the digital landscape we know today.

From a young age, Gates exhibited exceptional programming and computer science aptitude. Alongside his childhood friend, Paul Allen, he established Microsoft in 1975 to bring computers into every home and office. Their ground-breaking work led to the creation of the MS-DOS operating system, which laid the foundation for the subsequent success of Microsoft Windows.

Under Gates' leadership, Microsoft became a global powerhouse, introducing ground-breaking software and technologies that transformed how people interacted with computers. His visionary foresight and strategic business acumen propelled Microsoft to new heights, establishing it as one of the most dominant technology companies in the world.

However, Gates' impact extends beyond the realm of technology. Recognizing the importance of giving back, he dedicated much of his wealth and resources to philanthropy. Through the Bill and Melinda Gates Foundation, established in 2000, Gates has made substantial contributions to global health, education, and poverty alleviation initiatives, striving to make a positive and enduring impact on society.

Beyond his professional accomplishments, Gates is admired for his intellectual curiosity, insatiable appetite for knowledge, and passion for learning. His commitment to innovation and his dedication to improving the lives of others has solidified his status as an influential thought leader and role model for aspiring entrepreneurs and philanthropists worldwide.

This book focuses on the invaluable principles that have fuelled his extraordinary success. From co-founding Microsoft to becoming a prominent figure in technology and philanthropy, Gates has left an indelible mark on the business landscape.

Drawing inspiration from Gates' life and achievements, this book uncovers the core principles that have shaped his path to success. Through meticulous research and analysis, readers will gain insights into his relentless pursuit of innovation, unwavering determination, and unparalleled vision.

The book provides a guide, offering practical strategies and actionable steps from Gates' experiences. It reveals the power of embracing failure as a catalyst for growth, the importance of continuous learning, and the impact of fostering a strong work ethic. Moreover, it underscores the significance of collaboration, adaptability, and positively impacting society.

As readers delve into the success principles of Bill Gates, they will be inspired to redefine their path and overcome obstacles with resilience and purpose. By absorbing the wisdom from Gates' journey, readers can embark on their transformative quests and unlock their true potential.

❑

Contents

Success Can Be Deceptive

Success often instils a profound sense of accomplishment and self-assurance. When significant milestones are reached, or outstanding achievements are realized, it is natural to assume that the secret to success has been unlocked, rendering failure impossible. Unfortunately, this perception can lead to a stagnant mindset, discouraging further learning, adaptation, and innovation.

However, actual growth and wisdom are nurtured through encountering failures and setbacks. Failures are crucial stepping stones to success, compelling us to reassess our strategies, learn from our mistakes, and make necessary adjustments. They grant us resilience, humility, and the impetus for continuous improvement.

Bill Gates once said, “Success, as a teacher, can be deceptive, leading intelligent individuals to believe in their invincibility.” Hence, when success veils us in false security, we may overlook warning signs or resist change. The inclination to question our assumptions dwindles, the willingness to take risks diminishes, and we become trapped within outdated paradigms. Ultimately, this impedes our ability to innovate and adapt to an ever-changing world.

Having experienced both success and failure, Bill Gates believes that the lessons gleaned from failures surpass those derived solely from success. Failure offers a unique opportunity for introspection, growth, and transformation, whereas success can sometimes blind us to our flaws and restrict our potential.

Hence, it is imperative for intelligent individuals, irrespective of their past successes, to remain humble, curious, and receptive to new knowledge. Embracing failure as a catalyst for personal evolution, we must continuously challenge ourselves to improve, innovate, and create positive changes in the world.

It is essential to understand that success is not a destination but an ongoing journey. No matter how accomplished or achievement-oriented we may feel, there will always be new heights to reach, new skills to acquire, and new challenges to overcome. The moment we become complacent and believe we have reached the pinnacle of success is when we limit our growth potential.

Thus, by embracing failure, we open ourselves up to valuable opportunities for learning and improvement. Each setback presents a chance to reflect on our actions, analyse our decisions, and gain insights to guide us towards tremendous success. Failure teaches us resilience, adaptability, and the importance of perseverance in adversity. Perhaps this is why even after facing failures in school, Bill Gates still becomes one of the legendary entrepreneurs of today. Because he knew that a few defeats in life do not constitute his whole life; if anything, they help build the path to success.

In our pursuit of success, it is crucial to maintain a growth mindset that recognizes that failure is not the end but a stepping stone towards future accomplishments. This mindset encourages us to take calculated risks, embrace new ideas, and challenge conventional thinking. It empowers us to continuously seek knowledge, explore new avenues, and adapt to an ever-evolving world.

So, embrace failure as an integral part of our journey, not be deterred by setbacks, and remain humble in our successes, always seeking opportunities to learn and grow. By doing so, we can unlock our true potential, create positive change, and make a lasting impact in our lives and the lives of others. As the famous author of *Rich Dad, Poor Dad*, Robert Kiyosaki said, "Successful people do not fear failure but understand that it is necessary to learn and grow from them."

Lesson: *It is fine to celebrate success but it is more important to heed and learn from the lessons of failure.*

❑

Start Early

Starting to work on your ideas early in life is crucial because can shape the trajectory of your journey. It is a notion that holds immense power and potential, one that everyone should embrace with open arms.

When we embark on our ventures in youth, we are blessed with a unique advantage. The canvas of time stretches out before us, offering a generous expanse to explore, experiment, and bring our ideas to life. It is during these formative years that we possess a reservoir of energy, enthusiasm, and an insatiable thirst for knowledge.

By starting early, we tap into the boundless wellspring of creativity that resides within us. We are unburdened by the weight of conventional wisdom and the constraints of preconceived notions. Our minds are free to wander, unencumbered by the limitations that often arise as we grow older.

Moreover, the early pursuit of our ideas allows us to cultivate a mindset of resilience and determination. We become acquainted with the inevitable challenges and setbacks that accompany any endeavour. Through these experiences, we develop a tenacity that enables us to weather storms and navigate obstacles with grace.

The co-founder of Microsoft, Bill Gates understands the importance of starting early. This is the reason why he was only 13 years old when he began working with computers. He believes that when we start learning or practising something at an early point in life, we get moulded around it. When we begin working towards our dreams when we are young, then we become immune to criticism and discouraging opinions of people around us. Moreover, researches have proved that childhood days are the best period of time to inculcate new skills and habits.

Working on our ideas early grants us the freedom to fail, learn, and adapt. It is through this iterative process that we gain invaluable insights, refine our skills, and hone our craft. We gradually unravel the mysteries of our passions and find our unique voice in the symphony of life.

However, starting early is not merely about gaining a head start or achieving success at a young age. It is about nurturing our dreams, nurturing our sense of purpose, and nurturing the flame that burns within us. It is about building a foundation of experience and wisdom that will support us throughout our lives.

So, my dear friend, if you harbour dreams, if you possess ideas that stir your soul, do not hesitate. Seize this moment, harness the energy of youth, and embark on the journey that awaits you. Begin the pursuit of your ideas with resolve, unwavering determination and a steadfast belief in your potential. After all, we never know what future brings for us. It is unknown to all. Gates once said in an interview, "The Ebola epidemic can serve as an early wake-up call to get ready and be prepared. If we start now, we can be ready for the next epidemic." Thus, starting early in life will help you to be prepared for the unpredictable future.

Know that starting early is not a guarantee of instant success or a smooth path. There will be challenges, moments of doubt, and setbacks along the way. But it is through these trials that we grow, evolve, and become the architects of our own destiny. So, let us begin now. Let the fire within you burn brightly, and let the world bear witness to the remarkable creations that emerge from your early beginnings.

Lesson: *Begin working on your dreams early in life because the earlier you begin, the more ahead you will be to your competitors.*

❑

Embrace Patience

Patience is a key element to success. It is the ability to endure difficult circumstances, setbacks, and delays without losing hope or giving up. Patience allows us to stay focused on our goals, make better more sensible decisions, and persevere through challenges.

In today's fast-paced world, instant gratification has become the norm. We want quick results and immediate rewards, often neglecting the importance of patience. However, success rarely happens overnight. It requires consistent effort, time, and resilience.

Understanding this, Bill Gates advises everyone to have patience because great inventions do not happen in a day. Every valuable thing takes time to be formed. For instance, every lady's best-friend, diamonds take between 1 billion to 3.3 billion years' time to transform from carbon to a precious gem.

Even the great inventor and businessman, Thomas Edison advised people to have patience because it was patience that helped him become one of the renowned inventors of the world. It took him numerous attempts and thousands of experiments before he finally succeeded. On one instance Edison said, "I have not failed. I have just found 10,000 ways that won't work." Despite facing repeated failures, he remained patient and persistent, ultimately achieving a ground-breaking invention that revolutionized the world.

Hence why, Gates called patience a key element of success. He believes that patience is not merely a virtue but a crucial attribute for long-term achievements. In the business world, patience is essential for entrepreneurs and investors. Many successful business leaders have faced innumerable setbacks and obstacles along their journey. They understand that building a company or achieving financial success takes time. They patiently invest in their ideas, learn from failures, adapt their strategies, and persevere till they or attain reach their objectives. Gates did exactly the same when he patiently invested all his time to create the Windows line of operating systems, which is one of the prime products of his company Microsoft. Though it took him and his team longer than four years to develop Windows but now we cannot imagine our PCs without it.

Patience also helps us make better more informed decisions. Gates asserts that in a world driven by instant gratification, cultivating patience is essential for making wise decisions and enduring through challenges. When we rush into things impulsively, we are more likely to overlook critical details or make hasty choices. By cultivating patience, we can take the time to evaluate options, gather information, and consider the long-term consequences. This thoughtful approach increases our chances of making sound decisions that lead to success.

Patience not only helps us persist in the face of challenges but it also reflects the nature of our character. It is the reflection of our behaviour and mindset. Additionally, patience plays a significant and key role in our interactions with others. It fosters empathy, understanding, and the ability to actively listen. Patient individuals are more likely to give others the benefit of the doubt, allowing space for different perspectives and ideas. As the saying goes, "Patience is not the ability to wait, but to keep a positive attitude while waiting." So, inculcate the virtue of patience in your life if you want to become successful.

Lesson: *Patience is a key element to success, so embrace it.*

❑

Accept Life's Inequity

Adapting to life is a crucial aspect of personal growth and success. It is important to acknowledge that life is not always fair. We are all born with different circumstances, abilities, and opportunities. Not everybody starts off perfectly or with a golden spoon in their mouths. However, the key to overcoming these challenges is to adapt and accept life's inequities.

Adapting means recognising the hand you have been dealt and making the most of it. It involves embracing the reality that life may not always go the way we want it to, but that does not mean we cannot change it. We have the power to shape our own destinies and create the life we desire. Adapting to life's challenges requires a mindset of flexibility and resilience. It means being open to new possibilities and approaches when faced with obstacles. Instead of dwelling on the unfairness of circumstances, we can choose to focus on finding creative solutions and learning from our experiences. It also involves seeking support from others. We do not have to face life's challenges alone. Building a strong and firm network of relationships, seeking guidance from mentors, or seeking professional help can provide us with the resources and support we need to navigate difficult situations.

Hence why, Gates says, "Life is not fair; get used to it." Therefore, if you are out there waiting for the world to treat you in a certain manner and that does not appear to be the case, it is time to wake up and make the decision to take the best chance at life rather than giving up and being resentful or covering yourself in sackcloth to attract more sympathy.

Moreover, according to Gates, self-indulgence will not take care of your bills, support your family, or assist you with carrying on with the existence that you have consistently envisioned; taking the necessary steps to achieve your goals would, as would setting specific goals for yourself. You do not have to continue living a mediocre life because you are waiting for the world to turn out a certain way. Right now is an ideal opportunity to make a move and follow through with those things you have guaranteed yourself and your loved ones.

To adapt effectively, it is necessary to take personal responsibility and ownership of our lives. We must recognise that we are in control of our actions and choices. While there may be limitations and setbacks, our attitude, determination, and resilience can make a significant difference. No one else can live our lives for us. By taking charge, we can navigate through obstacles, seize opportunities, and make the necessary changes to improve our circumstances.

Adapting to life involves accepting that it may be unfair and not always favourable. However, by embracing this reality, taking personal responsibility, and making the necessary changes, we can shape our own destinies and create the life we desire. Remember, your future lies in your own hands, and it is up to you to manage and handle your own life. Life may seem unfair but this is no reason to give up on it. Accept it for what it is and make the best of it.

Lesson: *Life is not fair. Get used to it.*

❑

Be Your Own Boss

Bill Gates says, "Be your own boss as soon as possible because if you don't build your dream, someone else will hire you to build theirs." According to him, being your own boss is an incredibly empowering and fulfilling experience. It allows you to shape your own destiny, pursue your passions, and make a meaningful impact on the world. Gates himself became a boss at a young age. It provided him the opportunity to take absolute control over his destiny. However, to become your own boss requires a combination of ambition, determination, and strategic thinking to succeed.

To become your own boss as soon as possible, you need to cultivate a strong entrepreneurial mindset. This involves embracing risk-taking, learning from failures, and constantly seeking new opportunities. Being your own boss means being the driving force behind your success, and that requires resilience and adaptability in the face of challenges.

It is crucial to develop a deep understanding of the industry or field you wish to enter. This knowledge will provide a solid foundation for your ventures and help you identify gaps or inefficiencies that can be addressed with innovative solutions. By becoming an expert in your chosen area, you can position yourself as a valuable asset and gain a competitive edge.

According to Gates, becoming your own boss is important because it grants you the freedom to make decisions and set your own direction. You get the autonomy to choose the projects you work on, the people you collaborate with, and the overall vision for your business. This level of freedom allows you to align your work with your personal values and priorities. Furthermore, when you are your own boss, you have the opportunity to pursue your passions and work on projects that truly excite and stimulate you.

Finally, remember that being your own boss is not just about personal success but also about making a positive impact on society. As an entrepreneur, you have the power to create opportunities for yourself and for others. Gates has often emphasised the importance of job creation and economic empowerment. Being your own boss allows you to build a team, provide employment opportunities, and make a positive lasting impact on the community and economy.

Though Gates does advise people to become their own

boss as soon possible, he also cautions them to be wise and thoughtful while making decisions in business. He advises aspiring entrepreneurs to take the time to learn from mentors, gain valuable industry insights, and develop a robust network of support. Building these foundations will help navigate the challenges and complexities that come with being your own boss.

Remember, we have only two options in life—become your own boss or work for one. Becoming your own boss means embracing the essence of who you are, your passions, and your unique talents. It is an opportunity to sculpt your work around the very fabric of your being, aligning your purpose with your daily pursuits. No longer will you be confined to fit within someone else's mould; instead, you can paint your own masterpiece on the canvas of your professional journey. As someone once said, "Happiness is working on your terms and being your own boss."

Lesson: *Be your own boss as soon as possible because if you do not build your dream, someone else will hire you to build theirs.*

❑

Be a Reader

Reading is an essential skill that opens up a world of knowledge and opportunities for personal growth. It allows individuals to access a vast array of information. Books, articles, and other written materials serve as repositories of knowledge accumulated over centuries. By immersing oneself in the written world, one can explore diverse perspectives, learn about different cultures, and gain insights from experts in various fields. Reading expands one's understanding of the world, offering a broader and more comprehensive knowledge base.

Hence, Gates says, "People cannot become truly knowledgeable without being excellent readers." He believes that reading fosters critical thinking and intellectual development. Through reading, we learn to analyze, evaluate, and synthesize information, thus enhancing our ability to make well-informed decisions and contribute meaningfully to discussions and debates.

Reading also enhances language skills and communication abilities. The more we read, the more we are exposed to well-structured sentences, new vocabulary, and diverse writing styles. This exposure not only improves our own writing and speaking abilities but also helps us understand others better. Effective communication is crucial for sharing knowledge, collaborating with others, and influencing positive change.

For Gates, reading is a gateway to new worlds, a portal that transports us beyond the confines of our own experiences. It is a key that unlocks the treasures of knowledge, wisdom, and human creativity. Furthermore, he believes that reading is the fuel that feeds our intellectual curiosity. To him it is a never-ending feast that nourishes our minds and propels us towards constant growth and self-improvement. In the pages of books, he finds solace, inspiration, and the catalyst for his own remarkable journey of innovation and success.

Once, in an interview Gates said, "I spend a lot of time reading. Whether I am at home or on the road. I always have a stack of books I am looking forward to read." On another instance, he said, "You do not really start getting old till you stop learning. Every book teaches me something new or helps me see things differently." Thus, proving that reading is an integral part of every successful person.

In addition, reading promotes empathy and emotional intelligence. When we read novels, biographies, or even news articles, we encounter different characters and their experiences. This exposure to diverse narratives helps us develop empathy, enabling us to understand and relate to others' perspectives and emotions. Empathy is essential for effective collaboration, problem-solving, and building meaningful relationships, both personally and professionally.

Reading also plays a pivotal role in enhancing imagination and creativity. When we immerse ourselves in a book, we are transported to new worlds, whether they are fantastical realms or realistic settings. Through vivid descriptions and engaging storytelling, reading stimulates our imagination and allows us to envisage the places, characters, and events within the narrative.

Furthermore, reading serves as a gateway to personal growth and self-reflection. As we study various genres and literary works, we encounter characters who face challenges, embark on journeys of self-discovery, and overcome obstacles. Their stories often mirror aspects of our own lives, prompting introspection and deepening our understanding of ourselves.

In conclusion, the more you read, the more you will learn. The more you learn, the more you will realise that everything you need to become successful is within your reach.

Lesson: *People cannot be truly knowledgeable without being excellent readers.*

❑

Enter into Partnerships

Bill Gates holds a deep appreciation for the profound impact of partnerships, both on a personal and professional level. His idea of entering into partnerships reflects a belief in the transformative power of collaboration and the boundless potential that arises when individuals and organisations join forces. Gates sees partnerships as a source of inspiration and shared purpose.

Partnerships evoke a sense of excitement and anticipation in everyone, igniting a fire within their soul. It is through partnerships that Gates finds the motivation to push boundaries, take risks, and achieve audacious goals that would be impossible to accomplish alone. Gates has always been fond of forming partnerships with people from distinct industries and fields—people who hold influencing and high positions.

The reason why Gates enjoyed forming partnerships is because it provides him with ample and abundant new opportunities and the chance to learn from other successful people in different fields. Gates recognises the unique expertise and insights that top leaders bring to the table. Their extensive experience and track record of success can offer valuable guidance and mentorship, fuelling personal growth and pushing the boundaries of what is possible. By aligning with these exceptional individuals, Gates sees an opportunity to learn from their wisdom, tap into their networks, and leverage their expertise to drive progress in his own endeavours.

In an interview, when asked about the reason behind Microsoft's success, Gates said, "Our success has really been based on partnerships formed from the very beginning." While talking about partnerships, one should remember that in business, you work with many accomplices. Although you may partner with clients and vendors regularly, your partnerships with your company's other leaders are arguably the most significant."

One of the most famous partnerships of Bill Gates with his company's leaders is with Steve Ballmer. They both worked together at Microsoft for about 33 years. Though they have now parted ways, their partnership was responsible to make Microsoft a billion-dollar company that it is today. This shows how great partnerships could bring you the success that you desire.

Moreover, partnering with the right individuals or organisations brings together diverse skill sets, knowledge, and experience. It allows companies to tap into new perspectives, innovative ideas, and specialised expertise. Collaborating with partners who complement your strengths can lead to improved problem-solving, enhanced creativity, and more effective decision-making.

As Steve Jobs once said, "Great things in business are never done by one person; they are done by a team of people." So, form alliances that will help you achieve great successes and turn yours dreams into your reality.

Lesson: *Form alliances with successful and wise people, who can provide you with new opportunities and help you learn new skills—people who will assist you in achieving your vision.*

❑

Do Not Fear Change

Change is a powerful force that sweeps through the fabric of our lives, evoking several emotions deep within our souls. It is a symphony of anticipation, exhilaration, and trepidation, all woven together in the tapestry of transformation. Change is inevitable. The world is constantly changing around us, nothing stays the same forever.

Change is important because it breathes vitality into stagnant routines and opens the door to new opportunities, experiences, and perspectives. It allows us to break free from the shackles of complacency and mediocrity. Without change, we risk stagnation and missed opportunities. It is through change that we evolve, adapt, and respond to the ever-evolving world around us. It enables us to keep pace with advancements, whether they be technological, societal, or personal, and empowers us to navigate the complexities of our lives with grace and resilience.

Hence why, Bill Gates advises us to never fear change because it is an opportunity for growth and improvement. He believes that in a rapidly evolving world, adaptation and agility are crucial. Change compels us to question the status quo, challenge conventional thinking, and seek new and novel ways of doing things. It is through this process of change that breakthrough innovations can emerge, paving the way for advancements that have the potential to change lives and reshape entire industries.

According to Gates, people always fear change because for everyone an unknown territory will always seem dangerous. He expressed it aptly when he said, "People always fear change. They feared electricity when it was invented, didn't they?" The reason behind this fear was that the idea of electricity was a revolutionary concept that challenged the existing way of life. People were accustomed to gas lamps and candles, and the prospect of a new, invisible force that could potentially cause harm or disrupt their daily routines was unsettling. In this case, the fear of electricity stemmed from concerns about safety, the impact on traditional industries, and the disruption of established social norms.

Therefore, it is essential to remember that change is a part of our life and though it may sometimes seem forbidding and uncertain, it can lead to progress, innovation, and positive outcomes. Gates understands that change can be disruptive and may provoke resistance. However, he encourages embracing these moments of discomfort as opportunities for growth and learning. He believes that by embracing change and pushing through the initial discomfort, we can unlock new possibilities, expand our horizons, and achieve outcomes that were once unimaginable.

Remember as John Rim, the CEO of Samsung, once observed, "Your life does not get better by chance, it gets better by change." So, welcome change with open arms because you may never know what positive outcomes it may bring you.

> **Lesson:** *Do not fear change but embrace it with welcoming arms.*

❑

Expectations Manifest

Bill Gates says, "Expectations are a form of first-class truth. If people believe it, it is true." He understands that the beliefs and expectations we hold can shape our reality and influence the outcomes we experience.

Gates recognises that by envisaging and setting high expectations, individuals can motivate themselves to strive for excellence and achieve remarkable results. He believes that when we have a clear vision of what we want to accomplish and hold steadfast to those expectations, we create a powerful intention that drives our actions and decisions.

The concept of expectations manifesting refers to the phenomenon where our beliefs and expectations shape the outcomes and experiences we encounter in our lives. It suggests that what we anticipate and hold in our minds has the potential to become our reality. For instance, when we have positive expectations and maintain a hopeful outlook, then it creates a ripple effect that attracts opportunities, positive circumstances, and the realisation of our desired outcomes. On the other hand, negative expectations can inadvertently attract undesirable situations or hinder and impede our progress.

According to Gates, to harness the power of manifesting expectations, it is important to cultivate a mindset that aligns with our desired outcomes. This involves visualising success, maintaining a positive outlook, and taking actions that support our goals. By doing so, we can increase the likelihood of experiencing the outcomes we envisage.

However, it is worth noting that expectations manifesting is not solely reliant on positive thinking or wishful thinking. It requires a combination of focused intention, concerted efforts, and adaptability. While expectations play a role, they need to be supported by actions, perseverance, and a willingness to adapt to changing circumstances.

Gates insisted that by setting high standards, aligning them with perseverance and dedication, and maintaining a growth mindset, individuals can unleash their potential, accomplish extraordinary feats, and create a reality that aligns with their envisioned expectations. As the renowned comedian, Jim Carrey said, “Our intention is everything. Nothing happens on this planet without it. not a single purpose has ever been accomplished without intention.”

Therefore, clearly define your expectations, goals and desired outcomes. Then align your thoughts, emotions and actions with your expectations. Remember, manifestation is a process that takes time and requires patience. Trust that the universe or the forces at work, will align in your favour. Avoid forcing outcomes or becoming discouraged by delays or setbacks. Trust in the timing and have patience throughout the manifestation journey.

Lesson: *Expectations are a form of first-class truth. If people believe it, it is true.*

❑

Do Not Whine or Complain About Your Mistakes

Mistakes and failures are an inherent part of human experience that holds profound significance in our journey of growth and development. They serve as invaluable teachers, offering insights and lessons that shape our understanding, resilience, and personal evolution.

Mistakes, often accompanied by a sense of disappointment or frustration, provide us with opportunities for self-reflection and self-improvement. They reveal our vulnerabilities, weaknesses, and areas that require attention and growth. Rather than viewing mistakes as failures, it is essential to see them as stepping stones towards wisdom and progress.

Gates believes that mistakes and failures are inevitable in the journey of personal and professional growth. Rather than allowing them to hinder progress or dampen your spirit, he encourages people to analyse and understand the lessons they offer. By reflecting on what went wrong, identifying areas for improvement, and adjusting strategies accordingly, individuals can turn setbacks into catalysts for future success.

Moreover, Gates emphasises the significance of resilience and perseverance a diligence in the face of failure. He believes that the ability to bounce back, learn from mistakes, and keep moving forward is essential for achieving one's goals. By maintaining a positive mindset, embracing the lessons learned, and adapting approaches, individuals can continue to pursue their aspirations with renewed determination.

Gates also stresses the importance of fostering a culture that encourages learning from mistakes within organisations. He advocates an environment where employees feel safe to take risks, experiment, and learn from failures without fear of judgment or retribution. By cultivating a culture of continuous learning and improvement, businesses can foster innovation and derive long-term success.

Once in an interview, Gates said, "Learning from mistakes and constantly improving products is a key in all successful companies." According to Gates, mistakes foster resilience and determination. They test our mettle, challenging us to rise above setbacks, learn from our errors, and persevere. It is through mistakes that we build the resilience to overcome adversity, the strength to bounce back, and the courage to continue pursuing our dreams.

Moreover, mistakes are not indicative of our worth or abilities but rather opportunities for growth and self-discovery. They remind us of our humanity, teaching us humility, empathy, and the importance of continuous learning. By embracing our mistakes, we cultivate a growth mindset that embraces challenges, fuels innovation, and embraces the transformative power of perseverance.

Remember that life's greatest lessons are usually learned at the worst times and from the worst mistakes. So, stop deploring or protesting about your mistakes. Instead, heed significant lessons from them and empower yourself to become better, stronger and wiser individuals. Let mistakes and failures be your stepping stones on the path of growth and fulfilment.

Lesson: *Do not whine and complain about mistakes, learn from them.*

❑

Life is the Best Teacher

Life, with its vast array of experiences and lessons, stands as the ultimate teacher. It holds within its embrace the power to impart wisdom, shape character, and guide us on a journey of growth and self-discovery.

Through the triumphs and challenges, we encounter, life presents us with invaluable opportunities to learn, adapt, and evolve. It teaches us lessons that textbooks cannot convey and provides us with first-hand knowledge that goes beyond mere theory. Life's teachings are practical, profound, and deeply personal, tailored to our individual journeys.

According to Gates, regardless of the number of books you read and the number of tests you take, nothing from college or school can appropriately set you up for life in reality. Real-life jobs and bosses do not just involve you studying and them teaching you. Instead, it involves real-life work that you need to carry out, otherwise, you will have to face the consequences.

Gates emphasises the importance of embracing diverse experiences and seeking out new challenges. He encourages individuals to step outside their comfort zones, engage with different cultures, and immerse themselves in unfamiliar situations. Through these experiences, Gates believes we can broaden our horizons, gain a deeper understanding of the world, and cultivate a more comprehensive perspective.

The beauty of life as a teacher lies in its ability to offer continuous education. It does not confine learning to a specific time frame or limit it to a particular setting. Instead, it unfolds a lifelong curriculum that encourages exploration, curiosity, and a thirst for knowledge. Every day presents an opportunity to learn, to grow, and to expand our understanding of the world and ourselves.

For Gates, life is the ultimate teacher because it provides us with endless opportunities for growth, learning, and transformation. It is a lifelong journey that invites us to continuously expand our minds, deepen our understanding, and cultivate a sense of purpose. As we navigate the intricacies of existence, we must embrace life's teachings with open hearts and open minds, for they hold the key to unlocking our true potential and living a fulfilling and meaningful life.

Therefore, remember that life is a great teacher because it will keep repeating its lesson till you learn your lesson. Moreover, it teaches things that no one else can.

Lesson: *Life is the best teacher. It gives lessons after taking the exam.*

❑

Be a Team Player

Teamwork holds immense significance in various aspects of life, whether it is in the workplace, sports, or personal endeavours. Engaging in tasks and pursuing goals with the assistance and involvement of others can lead to more fruitful outcomes and a richer experience. Gates believes that our journey towards success becomes more meaningful and fruitful when we choose not to tread the path alone. Through his remarkable career, Gates adeptly fostered a culture that attracted and nurtured the best and brightest individuals, recognising the pivotal role they play in achieving scalable success.

According to Gates, being a team player means actively contributing to the collective effort, valuing diverse perspectives, and fostering an environment of trust and respect. It involves recognising that no individual possesses all the necessary skills and knowledge to solve complex problems or bring about meaningful change on their own. He believes that by working and collaborating together as a team, leveraging the strengths of each member, and encouraging open communication, extraordinary results can be achieved. Gates himself has often attributed Microsoft's success to the collective efforts of a highly collaborative and talented team.

For Gates, a dedicated team is one that acts with the same unity of purpose and focus as a well-motivated individual. On doing things alone, he says, "Don't do it alone. You are better when you have got the right people around you." Being a team player is of utmost importance in any setting, as it enables individuals to work unitedly towards shared goals, leverage each other's strengths, and achieve remarkable outcomes. By actively participating in a team, individuals foster a spirit of cooperation, effective communication, and mutual respect. Being a team player promotes unity, synergy, and a sense of belonging, creating an environment where diverse perspectives are valued and harnessed for innovation and problem-solving.

Team work encourages individuals to put aside personal ego and prioritise the collective success, contributing their unique skills and talents to the greater good. Moreover, being a team player cultivates important interpersonal skills, such as empathy, active listening, and conflict resolution, facilitating harmonious relationships and fostering a positive and productive work or social environment. Ultimately, the power of teamwork lies in its ability to bring people together, capitalise on their collective strengths, and achieve exceptional results that surpass individual capabilities.

Furthermore, Gates emphasises the importance of embracing constructive feedback and being open to different viewpoints. He believes that by creating an environment where everyone feels comfortable sharing their ideas, concerns, and suggestions, teams can make more informed decisions and drive continuous improvement. Therefore, he encourages leaders to set clear goals, provide guidance, and empower team members to take ownership of their responsibilities. By creating an inclusive and supportive environment, leaders can inspire individuals to perform at their best and achieve exceptional outcomes collectively.

Lesson: *Do not do things alone. Team work gives you an exceptional outcome as you can achieve better results when you work with people who have the same goal as yourself.*

❑

Be Committed

The state or quality of being staunch, loyal, and accountable to a particular cause, goal, or relationship is called commitment. It provides the necessary motivation and determination to work towards and achieve goals. It helps individuals stay focused, persevere through challenges, and overcome obstacles along the way.

Bill Gates, the co-founder of Microsoft and a prominent philanthropist, has often spoken about the importance of commitment in achieving success. Gates believes that commitment is a crucial trait for accomplishing goals and making a lasting and enduring impact on the world.

According to Gates, single-minded devotion is not merely about making promises or setting goals; it is about following through with action and persevering despite obstacles. He emphasises the need for dedication and consistency in pursuing one's objectives, even in the face of setbacks or failures.

Gates also highlights the significance of long-term commitment. He believes that meaningful progress requires sustained effort over time. He encourages individuals to stay focused on their goals, continuously learn and adapt, and remain dedicated to their chosen path, regardless of how challenging it may be.

Commitment holds immense importance because it reflects an individual's fervent or wholehearted determination and resolve to see their vision through, regardless of the obstacles or setbacks they may encounter along the way. For instance, Bill Gates's commitment to his vision of bringing a computer to every desk and home has had a transformative impact on the world. Despite facing numerous challenges, Gates remained focused and resilient, never wavering from his mission. His total commitment led to the establishment of Microsoft, a technology giant that revolutionised the computer industry and propelled society into the digital age. Witnessing such dedication is truly admirable and serves as a powerful reminder of the impact that commitment can have.

As important as personal commitment is, Bill Gates also lays emphasis on the importance of collective commitment to solving global challenges. He believes that governments, organisations, and individuals must come together and commit resources, expertise, and innovation to address issues such as poverty, disease, and climate change. Gates himself has demonstrated this commitment through his philanthropic work, particularly in the areas of global health and education. Regarding commitment, he once said, "Great organisations demand a high level of commitment by the people involved."

The reasons why commitment is vital in an individual's life is because it builds resilience, enabling individuals to bounce back from failures and setbacks. It encourages them to learn from their mistakes, adapt their strategies, and keep moving forward despite difficulties. Also, it fosters a sense of accountability and reliability. When individuals commit to a task or responsibility, they are more likely to fulfil their obligations and meet expectations, earning trust and respect from others.

Furthermore, as worthwhile endeavours require time and sustained effort, commitment helps individuals stay committed to their pursuits over the long term, even when initial progress may be slow or challenging. This dedication increases the chances of achieving lasting success. Additionally, commitment promotes personal growth and development. It pushes individuals out of their comfort zones, encourages them to acquire new skills and knowledge, and enables them to realise their full potential. Further, commitment empowers individuals to make a positive impact on the world. By dedicating themselves to causes larger than themselves, such as philanthropy, social justice, or environmental sustainability, committed individuals can effect meaningful change and contribute to the greater good and well-being.

Therefore, always remember to achieve success only having an interest in a particular goal will not help you. Instead, being committed to your goal will definitely get you results. So, stay committed to your goals, vision, or dreams.

Lesson: *Commitment is essential because it drives goal achievement, fosters resilience, promotes accountability, enables long-term success, facilitates personal growth, strengthens relationships, and empowers individuals to make a positive impact on the world.*

❑

Be Passionate

Being passionate about your goals is crucial for several reasons because it provides the fuel and motivation needed to pursue your goals with enthusiasm and dedication. When you are genuinely passionate about what you want to achieve, you are more likely to invest the time, effort, and resources required to succeed. Passion keeps you engaged and excited, making the journey towards your goals more enjoyable and fulfilling.

Also, passion helps you to overcome obstacles and persevere in the face of challenges. When you encounter setbacks or encounter difficulties, your passion serves as a driving force that pushes you to keep going. It gives you the resilience and determination needed to learn from failures, adapt your strategies, and continue moving forward.

According to Gates, being passionate about what you do is essential because it brings energy and enthusiasm to your work. When you are truly passionate about a subject or a goal, you are more likely to invest the time and effort needed to excel in that area. Passion fuels the desire to learn, explore, and push boundaries, leading to creative solutions and breakthroughs.

Gates also highlights that passion helps individuals stay motivated and resilient in the face of challenges. When you are passionate about your work, setbacks and failures become learning opportunities rather than deterrents or curbs. Your passion drives you to recover, bounce back, adapt, and continue pursuing your goals, even when the going gets tough.

Furthermore, Gates believes that passion is contagious. When you are genuinely passionate about what you do, it inspires and influences others around you. Your enthusiasm becomes a catalyst for collaboration, attracting like-minded individuals who share your vision and want to contribute to the same cause.

In addition to personal fulfilment, Gates acknowledges that passion plays a crucial role in making a significant impact on the world. When you are passionate about addressing a particular problem or making a difference in a specific field, your dedication and drive can lead to ground-breaking innovations and transformative change.

However, Gates also stresses that passion alone is not enough. It must be coupled with knowledge, expertise, and a commitment to continuous learning. While passion provides the fuel, it is essential to develop a deep understanding of the subject matter and acquire the necessary skills to turn passion into tangible outcomes.

In conclusion, being passionate about your goals is important because it provides motivation, fuels resilience, drives innovation, attracts collaboration, and enhances personal fulfilment. When you combine your passions with your aspirations, you create a powerful force that propels you towards success and allows you to make a meaningful impact on your journey.

Lesson: *Passion is one extraordinary power that releases inventiveness, since, supposing that you are energetic about something, then you are more prepared to face challenges.*

❑

Be Proud of Who You Are

It is natural to feel disheartened when we perceive ourselves as not being as smart, rich, or talented as those we look up to or admire. However, it is important to remember that we are all born with different sets of abilities, strengths, and circumstances.

One of the keys to achieving success and personal fulfilment is to accept and embrace our individuality. Each person possesses a unique combination of skills, talents, and perspectives that can contribute to their own version of success. By recognising and appreciating these inherent qualities, we can develop a sense of self-worth and confidence that allows us to pursue our goals with determination and resilience.

Gates believes that understanding and appreciating one's own worth is crucial for personal growth, happiness, and success. According to him, valuing yourself starts with recognising your unique strengths, talents, and abilities. It involves acknowledging your accomplishments and the impact you have made, no matter how big or small. By recognising your own worth, you gain confidence and a positive self-image that can propel you forward in pursuing your goals. In fact, he once said, "Don't compare yourself with anyone in this world. If you do so, you are insulting yourself."

So, rather than focusing on what we lack compared to someone like oneself, it is crucial to shift our mindset towards recognising and harnessing our own strengths and potential. This self-awareness and self-acceptance lays the foundation for personal growth and success. When we start appreciating ourselves and the unique contributions we can make, we become more motivated and empowered to explore and develop our talents further.

Gates also emphasises the significance of self-care and self-compassion. He believes that taking care of your physical, mental, and emotional well-being is essential for maintaining a healthy sense of self-worth. By prioritising self-care, you not only nurture yourself but also ensure that you have the energy and resilience to tackle challenges and make a meaningful impact.

Moreover, Gates encourages individuals to set boundaries and prioritise their own needs and values. Valuing yourself means respecting your own time, opinions, and personal space. By setting boundaries, you establish a healthy balance in your personal and professional life, preventing burnout and fostering a sense of self-worth.

Additionally, Gates stresses the importance of continuous learning and growth. He believes that valuing yourself means investing in your own development and acquiring new skills and knowledge. By seeking opportunities for learning and personal growth, you enhance your self-worth and expand your potential to contribute to the world.

Furthermore, Gates encourages individuals to surround themselves with a supportive network of people who appreciate and value them. Building relationships with individuals who recognise your worth and uplift you can have a positive impact on your self-esteem and overall well-being.

So, rather than becoming frustrated by perceived disparities between ourselves and those we admire, let us embrace the reality that we are all born differently. Let us appreciate ourselves, our abilities, and the unique gifts we bring to the table. By doing so, we can embark on our own journeys to success, fuelled by confidence and the determination to make a positive impact in our own way.

Lesson: *Value yourself, do not let others define your worth.*

❑

Be Pleasant and Affable to Nerds

In a world that often values popularity, athleticism, and social prowess, it is essential to remember the importance of embracing and respecting individuals who may be labelled as "nerds." Bill Gates, the renowned co-founder of Microsoft and one of the most influential figures in the tech industry, has consistently advocated for treating nerds with kindness and recognising their immense contributions to society. Gates firmly believes that being nice and pleasant to nerds is not only a matter of basic human decency but also crucial for fostering innovation, progress, and ultimately, a better world.

One of the key reasons why Bill Gates advocates kindness towards nerds is their unparalleled capacity for innovation. Nerds, often characterised as individuals with an intense passion for technology, science, or intellectual pursuits, possess a unique ability to think critically and solve complex problems. Their dedication to knowledge and expertise in their respective fields enables them to develop ground-breaking ideas and solutions that have the potential to revolutionise industries and improve people's lives.

Gates himself, as a self-proclaimed nerd, recognises the importance of supporting and encouraging these individuals. He understands that by fostering an environment where nerds are valued and respected, their innovative potential can be fully realised. The breakthroughs achieved by nerds, whether in the realm of technology, medicine, or any other field, have the power to transform societies and tackle some of humanity's most pressing challenges.

Moreover, Bill Gates emphasises the need for society to move beyond stereotypes and embrace diversity. Nerds often face social exclusion, ridicule, or marginalisation due to their interests and passions, which may deviate from mainstream norms. Gates asserts that valuing and respecting nerds is a step towards embracing diversity and inclusivity. By appreciating individuals for their unique talents, irrespective of social conventions, we create a more tolerant and accepting society that encourages everyone to pursue their passions.

Bill Gates also highlights the long-term economic benefits of nurturing a culture that values nerds. In an increasingly digital world, where technology permeates every aspect of our lives, the demand for individuals with technical skills is rapidly growing. By recognising the value of nerds and investing in their education and development, we ensure a skilled workforce that can drive technological advancements and stimulate economic growth. Gates firmly believes that by harnessing the potential of nerds and providing them with opportunities, we can foster innovation-led economies that benefit everyone.

Additionally, Gates acknowledges that being considerate or sympathetic to nerds goes beyond immediate benefits; it is a matter of promoting empathy and compassion. Just as it is crucial to be kind to individuals with different abilities, backgrounds, or interests, treating nerds with respect demonstrates our capacity for empathy. By acknowledging and appreciating the unique contributions of nerds, we create a more compassionate society that values the diversity of human intellect and nurtures the talents of all individuals.

In conclusion, Bill Gates passionately advocates for being sympathetic to nerds, highlighting their capacity for innovation, the need for inclusivity, economic benefits, and the promotion of empathy. He put it aptly when he said, "Be nice to nerds. Chances are you will end up working for one." By embracing and respecting nerds, we create an environment that encourages their contributions and empowers them to reach their full potential. Gates believes that by doing so, we can unleash a wave of innovation, drive economic growth, and foster a more compassionate and inclusive society.

Ultimately, being more considerate to nerds is not just an act of kindness; it is a step towards building a better future for all.

Lesson: *Be pleasant and affable to nerds because you never know, you may end up working for them.*

❑

Share Your Knowledge

"Knowledge is power" is a widely recognised phrase that emphasises the immense value and influence of knowledge. Knowledge equips individuals with information, insights, and skills that can be applied to solve problems, make informed decisions, and achieve desired goals. It enables individuals to adapt, innovate, and seize opportunities, ultimately leading to personal growth and success. Hence, Bill Gates has always advocated for the power of knowledge and the importance of sharing it.

Throughout his career, Gates has emphasised the transformative potential of sharing knowledge, not only in the tech industry but also in addressing global challenges and creating a more equitable world. His commitment to sharing knowledge stems from his belief that knowledge is a valuable resource that should be accessible to all, as it has the potential to drive innovation, empower individuals, and bring about positive change. He even once said, "Power comes not from knowledge kept but from knowledge shared."

One of the key reasons why Gates promotes the sharing of knowledge is its role in fostering innovation. Gates firmly believes that innovation thrives when knowledge is freely shared and collaboration is encouraged. By sharing knowledge and ideas openly, barriers to progress are dismantled, and new discoveries can be made. Gates himself has been an advocate for open-source software and has actively supported initiatives that promote the sharing of code and technical knowledge. He understands that when people are free to build upon the knowledge of others, breakthroughs happen more rapidly, and society as a whole benefit from the collective wisdom and expertise.

Furthermore, Gates recognises that sharing knowledge is a powerful tool for empowering individuals, particularly those in disadvantaged communities. He strongly believes in the democratising potential of knowledge, that by providing access to information and education, people can acquire the skills and knowledge necessary to improve their lives. Gates and his foundation have invested heavily in initiatives aimed at improving access to education and technology, particularly in underserved regions. By sharing knowledge, Gates envisages a world where everyone, regardless of their background or circumstances, has the opportunity to reach and attain their full potential and contribute meaningfully to society.

Another critical aspect of Gates' advocacy for sharing knowledge is its role in addressing global challenges. Gates has been at the forefront of efforts to combat infectious diseases, poverty, and climate change. He recognises that sharing knowledge is essential in finding innovative solutions to these complex problems. Gates has been a strong proponent of data sharing, collaboration among scientists and researchers, and the open exchange of information in the pursuit of global health and development. He believes that by pooling knowledge and resources, we can accelerate progress and make significant strides towards a more sustainable and equitable future.

Moreover, Gates acknowledges that sharing knowledge is not limited to the realm of science and technology. It extends to fields such as policymaking, business, and philanthropy. Gates has been and continues to be vocal about the importance of transparency in government and organisations, advocating for the sharing of information to foster accountability and better decision-making. He believes that by sharing knowledge and insights, we can collectively address societal challenges, make informed choices, and drive positive change.

Remember, giving or receiving some information from others is not the goal or objective of knowledge sharing. That only applies to sharing information. When people genuinely want to assist one another in developing new capacities for action, knowledge sharing occurs. It involves creating a learning system. So, share your knowledge with others and help educate them to become a wiser and knowledgeable individuals.

Lesson: *Knowledge is a tressure that expands when shared with others.*

❑

Leaders Empower Others

In a world transformed by progress and the recognition of interconnectedness, the concept of leadership has undergone a profound evolution. Traditional notions of leadership centred around asserting authority and control no longer hold the same weight. Instead, the most influential leaders of this new era are those who focus on empowering the people around them.

To empower others is to provide them with the resources, support, and guidance they need to thrive. It requires creating a culture of trust and collaboration, where every voice is valued and every contribution is recognised. In this environment, the unique skills and ideas of each individual can contribute to finding innovative solutions to the challenges we face.

Bill Gates has long believed that true leaders are those who empower others. This is why, he says, "As we look ahead into the next century, leaders will be those who empower others." He understands the importance of nurturing and enabling the potential of individuals to drive positive change and create a lasting and enduring impact.

According to Gates, leaders who empower others prioritise the growth and development of their team members. They recognise the unique talents and abilities of individuals and provide them with the necessary resources, guidance, and support to reach their full potential. By empowering others, leaders create an environment that fosters innovation, collaboration, and personal growth.

Gates stresses that empowering others is not about exerting control or micromanaging, but rather about creating a culture of trust and autonomy. Effective leaders trust their team members to make decisions, take risks, and learn from their experiences. They provide a safe space where individuals feel empowered to voice and express their ideas, share their perspectives, and contribute meaningfully to the collective goals of the organisation or community.

Moreover, Gates believes that empowering others is essential for building strong and resilient teams. When individuals feel empowered, they are more engaged, motivated, and committed to the shared vision and goals. Empowered team members take ownership of their work, demonstrate initiative, and are more likely to go above and beyond in their efforts. This not only leads to better outcomes but also cultivates a positive and inclusive work culture that attracts and retains top talent.

Bill Gates also recognises that empowering others goes beyond the immediate benefits within an organisation or team. It has a ripple effect on society as a whole. When leaders empower individuals, they enable them to contribute their unique perspectives, skills, and ideas to address complex social challenges. Empowered individuals become agents of change, driving innovation, and making a positive impact in their communities.

Furthermore, Gates believes that empowering others is a catalyst for long-term sustainability. By investing in the growth and development of individuals, leaders create a pipeline of future leaders who will continue to empower others. This creates a cycle of empowerment, where individuals pass on or transmit their knowledge, skills, and opportunities to the next generation, ensuring a legacy of positive impact and leadership.

Looking ahead, it is clear that the power of empowerment holds the key to building a brighter future. Leadership is no longer about control but about uplifting others. By embracing this philosophy, we can create a world where everyone is inspired to contribute their best and work towards common goals.

Lesson: Empowering others to do things they did not think were possible is at the heart of leadership.

❑

Actions Are a Must

While having a vision is essential and often serves as a starting point for progress, the actions ultimately bring ideas to life and yield tangible results. By translating vision into action, dreams can grow and become energised.

Ideas and visions provide inspiration and direction but are only the first step in the journey towards accomplishment. Through deliberate actions, perseverance, and commitment, visions are transformed into tangible outcomes. Action is what bridges the gap between aspirations and actual achievements.

In the absence of action, visions remain mere fantasies or wishful thinking. They only hold value if backed by concrete steps and a commitment to making them a reality. Ideas and dreams can become hollow without action and fail to make a meaningful impact. Being a genius himself, Gates understands that a vision with proper execution is merely daydreaming and needs more power to create significant impact or drive substantial change.

Gates understands that execution involves taking deliberate actions, making strategic decisions, and implementing plans to bring a vision to life. It requires careful planning, attention to detail, and a relentless focus on translating ideas into practical outcomes. Without the discipline and determination to execute, a vision remains nothing more than an abstract concept or a lofty aspiration.

Moreover, Gates highlights that execution separates successful individuals and organisations from those who merely dream. The ability to convert ideas into actions and navigate the challenges and complexities along the way leads to a real and decisive impact. Without execution, even the most brilliant and inspiring vision remains confined to the realm of imagination, unable to make a meaningful difference in the world.

Gates himself is known for his exceptional execution skills. His success in co-founding Microsoft and leading it to become one of the most influential tech companies in the world is a testament to his commitment to turning vision into action. Gates has consistently demonstrated a relentless pursuit of excellence, focusing on the execution of innovative ideas to create ground-breaking products and solutions. Regarding actions, he once said, "I was fortunate to be in the right place at the right time. But many others were also in the same place. The difference was that I took action."

Therefore, you must work on your dreams to achieve success and stand out from the rest. Furthermore, by actively working towards executing our ideas, we uphold the moral value of transforming our intentions into tangible outcomes. We demonstrate our commitment to turning ideas into reality through deliberate action, harnessing their potential to create lasting change.

Remember, visions without actions lack the transformative power necessary to bring about change and achieve desired outcomes. While having a vision is important, dreams are realised through deliberate and consistent efforts. Taking action is essential for progress, learning, and ultimately turning aspirations into concrete achievements. As the renowned inventor Thomas Edison said, "Having a vision for what you want is not enough. Vision without execution is hallucination." So, take the necessary action to make your vision a reality.

Lesson: *Vision without execution is daydreaming.*

Focus on Unhappy Customers

Customers are the foundation of any business, as they play a vital role in its success and sustainability. They drive revenue generation, market demand validation, customer loyalty, and market differentiation. Customers directly contribute to a business's financial stability by purchasing its products or services, providing the necessary revenue for growth and operations. Their preferences, feedback, and purchasing behaviour help businesses understand market demand and validate the viability of their offerings.

While speaking to happy and satisfied customers is easy, understand and listen to those unhappy with your services or products. Instead of arguing with them and telling them they are wrong, learn from their feedback how to make their future customer experience more satisfactory. Please take into account every feedback they give you, as it will help you improvise your products or services as per your customer's needs.

This is the reason why; Bill Gates has always valued the opinions of dissatisfied customers. He says that focusing on unhappy customers is a crucial business strategy. He recognises that unhappy customers provide valuable feedback and insights that can drive innovation and lead to better customer experiences. By listening to and addressing the concerns of dissatisfied or discontented customers, businesses can identify areas for improvement, make necessary adjustments, and ultimately enhance the quality of their offerings.

Gates once said, "Your most unhappy customers are your greatest source of learning." Hence why, he acknowledges that unhappy customers have a strong influence on the reputation and growth of a business. With the advent of social media and online reviews, dissatisfied customers now have platforms to share their experiences and opinions, potentially reaching a vast audience. Addressing their concerns promptly and can effectively resolve immediate issues and contribute to building a positive brand image and customer loyalty.

Moreover, unhappy or discontented customers often highlight areas where competitors might gain an advantage. By paying attention to their feedback, businesses can identify market gaps and opportunities to outperform their rivals. Addressing the concerns of unhappy customers and exceeding their expectations can help enterprises to differentiate themselves and retain customers in a highly competitive market.

Also, by proactively seeking feedback, businesses can gain insights into customer pain points, preferences, and emerging needs. This knowledge can drive product development, service enhancements, and overall business strategies, ensuring ongoing relevance and customer satisfaction. Moreover, Gates believes that businesses are responsible for addressing customer concerns and ensuring fairness in their interactions. By prioritising the needs of unhappy or dissatisfied customers, businesses can demonstrate empathy, build trust, and contribute to a more equitable and customer-centric society.

Remember, as the American business magnate Sam Walton says, "There is only one boss, the customer. And he can fire everybody in the company from the chairman on down, simply by spending his money somewhere else."

Lesson: *Focus on unhappy dissatisfied customers because they provide the most valuable feedback.*

❑

Value Time

Time is a finite resource that defines the very essence of our existence. With only 24 hours a day and 365 days a year, our lives reflect the choices we make and how we use our time. Recognising life's brevity and valuing our time is crucial for personal growth and success.

Life is transient, and our time on this planet is limited. Each passing moment brings us closer to our ultimate destination. Realising the scarcity of time instils a sense of urgency to make the most of every opportunity. Every second that slips away is irreplaceable; thus, making conscious choices about how we spend our time becomes imperative.

According to Bill Gates, regardless of your money, buying back time is impossible. So, do not waste your working hours, and think wisely about how you spend every hour of your day. He believes that using time effectively is essential for personal and professional success. To make the most of his day, he divides the day into intervals of 5 minutes. Then, he jots down the results every 5 minutes and keeps tabs on his plans. This method helps him achieve better and more effective results. Even Elon Musk uses this same method to schedule his day.

Gates emphasises the significance of prioritising tasks and activities. In his view, it is crucial to focus on high-impact endeavours and allocate time and energy accordingly. Individuals can maximise their time and achieve greater productivity by identifying what truly matters and avoiding worthless time-wasting activities.

Efficiency and effectiveness are vital aspects of Gates's philosophy on time management. He advises working smartly and leveraging technology to streamline processes. By embracing efficient work strategies and eliminating unnecessary steps, individuals can accomplish more in less time, freeing up valuable resources for other endeavours.

Continuous learning is another aspect Gates emphasises when it comes to valuing time. He believes in acquiring knowledge and staying informed about advancements in various fields. Gates recognises that learning is an ongoing process, and by dedicating time to expand one's knowledge and skills, individuals can make informed decisions and adapt to changing circumstances more effectively.

Delegation and collaboration are also vital in Gates's perspective on time management. He stresses the importance of entrusting tasks to capable individuals and working collaboratively to leverage collective expertise. Delegating responsibilities allows individuals to focus on their strengths and create opportunities for innovation and shared success.

Furthermore, Gates believes in the value of reflection and finding balance. Taking time to pause, reflect, and recharge is essential for maintaining focus, perspective, and overall well-being. Gates understands the significance of self-care and maintaining healthy relationships, as these factors contribute to sustainable productivity and a fulfilling life.

As American businessman and author Harvey Mackay said, "Time is free, but it is priceless. You cannot own it, but you can use it. You cannot keep it, but you can spend it. Once you have lost it, you can never get it back." Therefore, be wise with your time. Please do not waste it away on meaningless and unproductive activities.

Lesson: *Time is more valuable than money; use it wisely.*

❑

Think Ahead

In a rapidly evolving world, where change is the only constant, the ability to think ahead has become more crucial than ever. Thinking ahead entails looking beyond the present and envisaging potential scenarios, challenges, and opportunities. It is a proactive approach that empowers individuals and organisations to navigate uncertainties, make informed decisions, and secure success. The forward-thinking progressive approach is essential for success in various aspects of life, including personal goals, business ventures, and problem-solving.

Throughout his career, Bill Gates has always emphasised the importance of forward-thinking in several areas, including technology, global development, and public health. He believes anticipating and preparing for the future is crucial for making meaningful progress and creating positive change. According to him, one key reason why thinking ahead is essential for success is that it allows individuals to be proactive rather than reactive. One can take early action to capitalise on advantages or mitigate risks by anticipating potential obstacles or opportunities. This mindset enables individuals to stay ahead of the curve and make informed decisions based on future possibilities rather than simply reacting to immediate circumstances. It helps individuals and organisations navigate uncertainties and adapt to changing conditions more easily.

Moreover, thinking ahead fosters strategic planning. It involves setting long-term goals, breaking them into actionable steps, and aligning present actions with future objectives. Individuals can make strategic choices and prioritise their efforts by having a clear vision of desired outcomes. Hence, it increases the chances of success and provides a roadmap for progress, enabling individuals to track their achievements and make necessary adjustments along the way.

Thinking ahead also promotes innovation and creativity. Individuals can identify emerging opportunities and develop innovative solutions by contemplating future trends and needs. It encourages individuals to explore new possibilities, challenge the status quo, and seek novel approaches to problem-solving. By thinking beyond the present and envisaging alternative futures, individuals can stay ahead of the competition and drive progress in their respective fields.

Understanding the need to think ahead, Gates and his team wonder how to satisfy their customers every day. Every day they would ask themselves, "How can we keep customers happy? How can we get ahead in innovation by this or that?" They have all long realised that if they do not get ahead in innovation, then somebody else will. Therefore, it is imperative to have a forward-thinking mindset because in the world of competition, you have to stand out amongst the crowd, or your competitors will take over the business lead.

Remember, thinking ahead is a valuable mindset for success as it enables individuals to be proactive, strategic, innovative, and resilient. So, plan your goals, anticipate obstacles, and take proactive steps to ensure success by thinking ahead.

Lesson: *A forward-thinking progressive mindset helps us move ahead in our professional and personal lives.*

❑

Dare to Take Risks

In the dynamic business world, taking risks has become fundamental for achieving growth and success. While risks may evoke apprehension, businesses must step outside their comfort zones and embrace calculated risks. Entrepreneurs and business owners willing to step out of their comfort zones and assume calculated risks often find themselves at the forefront of innovation and growth.

Taking risks is an integral part of business growth and success. By embracing calculated risks, organisations seize opportunities, drive innovation, overcome challenges, foster learning, and gain a competitive advantage. While risks come with uncertainties, the rewards can be substantial, propelling businesses to new heights and opening doors to unexplored possibilities. As businesses navigate the complex landscape of today's world, those willing to take risks are best positioned to adapt, thrive, and shape the future of their industries.

According to Gates, risk-taking in business refers to the deliberate pursuit of opportunities that involve uncertainty and the potential for both positive and negative outcomes. It consists in venturing into new territories, exploring uncharted markets, adopting disruptive technologies, and making bold decisions that challenge the status quo. He believes that you sometimes have to take significant risks to win big gains or profits. Success can never happen by sitting idle and taking small steps. You have to take a chance to make it big in life. Therefore, it is imperative to achieve success in business and life; you will have to take some risks because growth does not happen without it.

However, Gates does not advocate reckless risk-taking. Instead, he emphasises the importance of making calculated decisions. Gates encourages individuals to gather information, conduct thorough research, and weigh the potential risks and rewards before embarking on a particular venture. By carefully assessing the risks involved, individuals can make more informed decisions and increase their chances of success.

Gates has repeatedly taken risks in his life, resulting in significant lifestyle shifts for him. For instance, after graduating with a score of 1590 out of 1600 on his SAT, he stepped into Harvard Law School. But his passion for computers did not let him stay there for long. Soon after, he drastically dropped out of college to start a company with his friend, Paul Allen. Though a major risk then, his decision resulted in a significant change in his and life of others.

Remember, taking risks can lead to valuable learning experiences. Even if a chance does not yield the desired outcome, there is often a wealth of knowledge and insights gained from the process. Failures and setbacks can provide valuable lessons that help refine strategies, improve decision-making, and enhance overall business performance. Embracing these learning opportunities allows businesses to iterate and iterate again, ultimately increasing their chances of success.

So, remember the advice of Mark Zuckerberg, "The biggest risk is not taking any risk. In a world that is changing really quickly, the only strategy that is guaranteed to fail is not taking risks."

Lesson: *Risks are an indispensable part of success and growth.*

❑

Invest in the Poor

When most of us struggled to find our way, Bill Gates became a billionaire at 31. However, this achievement did not deter or pull him down. Instead, he changed his mind, and in 2000, he resigned as CEO of Microsoft to devote himself to philanthropy and established the Bill and Melinda Gates Foundation.

Bill took over as CEO and founder of Microsoft on March 13, 1986, when the company became a public company. On March 13, 2020, exactly 34 years later, Bill resigned from Microsoft's board of directors to devote his entire time to charitable causes. "This is to devote more time to philanthropic priorities, including global health and development, education, and my increasing engagement in addressing climate change,"

According to Gates, investing in people with low incomes is a moral imperative and an essential strategy for global development. He recognises that poverty is a complex issue with far-reaching implications, affecting individuals, communities, and entire nations. Gates understands that by investing in the poor, we can break the cycle of poverty and create a more equitable and prosperous world for everyone. He said, "We make the future sustainable when we invest in the poor, not when we insist on their suffering."

One of Gates' key arguments is that investing in people experiencing poverty is an investment in human capital. He believes that regardless of socio-economic status, every individual has untapped potential and can contribute meaningfully to society if given the right opportunities. By investing in healthcare, education, and economic empowerment, Gates aims to unlock the potential of people experiencing poverty and enable them to lead healthier, more productive lives. He sees these investments as crucial for fostering human development and reducing inequalities.

Moreover, Gates recognises the interconnectedness of global issues and the need for a comprehensive approach to address poverty. He understands that poverty is not an isolated problem but is intertwined with other challenges, such as disease, lack of access to education, and limited economic opportunities. Gates' philanthropic work tackles these interrelated issues holistically, seeking to create sustainable solutions that address the root causes of poverty.

Gates says, "The returns from investing in poor people are just as great as the returns from investing in the business world and have even more meaning." Hence, investing in the poor is a matter of social justice and an investment in human capital, economic growth, and sustainable development. Empowering the poor can create a more inclusive and prosperous world for everyone.

Lesson: *Invest in poor people so that they do not stay poor and we can all grow together.*

❑

The Power of Perseverance

Perseverance is a trait that Bill Gates holds in high regard and considers crucial for achieving greatness. Gates faced numerous challenges and setbacks throughout his remarkable journey, but his unwavering steadfast commitment and determination propelled him forward. His story serves as a powerful testament to the transformative power of perseverance and its significant impact on both personal and professional life.

Gates understood that success rarely comes without obstacles. In the early days of Microsoft, he encountered several hurdles, including fierce competition, technical difficulties, and financial constraints. However, instead of succumbing to these challenges, Gates persisted and remained focused on his goals. He believed setbacks were merely temporary roadblocks that perseverance could overcome.

One of the most notable examples of Gates' perseverance is Microsoft's journey to develop and establish the Windows operating system. Beyond personal achievements, Gates' persistence profoundly impacted Microsoft as an organisation. His unflinching resolute commitment to the company's mission and goals instilled a culture of resilience and determination. This culture of perseverance trickled down to employees, inspiring them to tackle challenges head-on and remain steadfast in their pursuit of excellence.

According to Gates, perseverance is the key to success in any endeavour. It is the ability to keep pushing forward, even in the face of challenges and setbacks. Even we can only use the most brilliant ideas and talents with perseverance. He learned early on that success rarely comes easily, and it requires an incredible amount of resilience and tenacity.

For him, perseverance is not just about working hard; it is about staying focused and committed when things do not go as planned. It is about adapting and learning from failures rather than letting them discourage you. Every setback is an opportunity to grow and improve.

Innovation and progress are often the result of perseverance. Some of history's greatest inventions and breakthroughs came from individuals who refused to give up. They kept pushing forward, believing in their ideas and ability to make a difference.

As the renowned actor Sylvester Stallone once said, "Going on one more round when you do not think you can, that is what makes all the difference in your life." So, embrace challenges, stay resilient, and never give up. Perseverance fuels success. Take action, persist, and achieve your dreams. Keep pushing forward, no matter what.

Lesson: *Perseverance is the key to success in any endeavour.*

❑

Do Not Make the Same Decision Twice

In our fast-paced world, decision-making is vital in both personal and professional spheres. However, revisiting decisions can be counterproductive, hindering execution and dampening motivation. Investing time and thought into our initial choices can enhance our effectiveness and maintain our drive to make decisions confidently.

According to Gates, we subject ourselves to many disadvantages when we continually revisit decisions. Firstly, reviewing decisions drains our time and energy. The resources spent on deliberating and reconsidering the same issue multiple times can be better allocated towards implementing the chosen path or addressing other pressing matters.

Additionally, the constant reopening of problems leads to indecisiveness, causing delays and missed opportunities. When we lack the conviction to finalise a decision, progress stagnates, and our growth potential diminishes.

Furthermore, revisiting decisions can negatively impact motivation. When we reopen issues frequently, it creates a sense of uncertainty and undermines our confidence in our judgment. This erosion of faith can be demoralising, leading to a lack of motivation to make decisions in the first place. If we anticipate that our choices will be continuously challenged, we may become reluctant to commit ourselves fully, resulting in a cycle of indecision and decreased productivity.

As Gates says, “Do not make the same decision twice. Spend time and thought to make a solid decision the first time so that you don’t revisit the issue unnecessarily. If you are too willing to reopen issues, it interferes not only with your execution but also with your motivation to make a decision in the first place. After all, why bother deciding an issue if it isn’t decided?” Hence, making solid decisions from the outset offers numerous benefits. By investing time and thought into our initial choices, we can ensure they are well-reasoned and based on a comprehensive understanding of the situation. Consequently, our decisions are more likely to sound and align with our goals and values.

Moreover, solid decisions instil a sense of confidence and clarity. When we take the time to make an informed choice, we develop trust in our decision-making abilities.

This confidence permeates our execution, enabling us to act decisively and assertively. It fosters a positive mindset and fuels motivation, as we are more likely to commit wholeheartedly to a decision we have thoroughly considered.

To avoid unnecessary revisits, cultivating a decisive decision-making mindset is crucial. This mindset involves embracing the responsibility and accountability that comes with making choices. By acknowledging that revisiting decisions can hinder progress and demotivate us, we can shift our focus towards making well-thought-out decisions initially.

Hence, adopting effective decision-making strategies can assist in developing this mindset. Gathering relevant information, seeking diverse perspectives, and considering potential consequences help us make informed choices. Furthermore, incorporating reflection into our decision-making process enables us to learn from past experiences and adjust for the future.

Therefore, let us strive to make informed decisions, maximising our productivity, motivation, and overall success in personal and professional endeavours.

Lesson: *Do not make the same decision twice. Spend time and thought to make a solid decision the first time so you do not unnecessarily revisit the issue.*

❑

Take a Break

In our fast-paced and demanding world, often taking a break falls by the wayside. We are caught up in the never-ending cycle of work, commitments, and responsibilities, neglecting the crucial need for downtime. However, understanding the art of taking a break is essential for our well-being and happiness. By embracing moments of rest and rejuvenation, we can find balance, enhance our productivity, and nurture our mental and emotional health.

In recent interviews and public statements, Bill Gates has discussed the importance of taking breaks and maintaining a healthy work-life balance. He believes that breaks are crucial for supporting creativity and avoiding burnout. In his life, Gates has frequently taken vacations to recharge and step away from work demands. He advocates for individuals to set aside time for leisure activities, hobbies, and spending quality time with loved ones. He asserts that people can achieve a more sustainable and fulfilling work-life equilibrium by doing so.

Additionally, Gates recognises the value of breaks for reflection and learning. He encourages individuals to engage in activities that broaden their horizons and stimulate their minds. Reading books, attending conferences, and participating in new experiences are among the ways he suggests expanding one's knowledge and perspective during the period away from work.

Furthermore, Gates acknowledges that breaks can be instrumental in preventing decision fatigue. He advises people to step back from the constant demands of decision-making to allow for mental rejuvenation. It will enable individuals to return to their responsibilities with greater clarity and focus.

While Gates acknowledges the importance of breaks, he also emphasises the significance of diligence and dedication. He believes that finding a balance between rest and effort is vital to achieving long-term success and positively impacting the world. As a philanthropist, Gates is deeply committed to addressing global challenges such as poverty, education, and healthcare, and he encourages others to find their areas of passion and contribute to the betterment and improvement of society.

In an interview, Gates once said, "Take time to nurture your relationships, to celebrate your successes, and to recover from your losses. Take a break when you need to. Take it easy on the people around you when they need it, too." Hence, breaks are also instrumental in nurturing and building relationships.

Nurturing and building relationships involves effective communication, active listening, and demonstrating empathy. Being present and attentive when interacting with loved ones is essential, fostering an environment where they feel heard and valued. We strengthen bonds and create lasting memories by dedicating quality time to our relationships.

Overall, occasionally taking a break is crucial for maintaining well-being, enhancing creativity, avoiding burnout, and nurturing relationships. Gates encourages individuals to prioritise leisure activities, engage in learning experiences, and spend quality time with loved ones. Individuals strive for personal and professional success by finding a healthy balance while contributing to the greater good.

Lesson: *Take breaks when needed to create a perfect work-life balance.*

❑

Everyone Needs a Mentor

In a world filled with endless possibilities and complex challenges, having a mentor for guidance can make a profound difference in our personal and professional lives. Bill Gates is a firm believer in the transformative power of mentorship. He asserts that mentors are crucial in shaping our journeys, providing wisdom, and helping us navigate the path to success.

Throughout his life and career, Gates has significantly benefited from the wisdom and guidance of mentors, and he believes this is a crucial aspect of personal and professional development. In an interview with CBC, he credited Warren Buffett for teaching him how to deal with difficult situations and have a long-term mindset. According to him, everyone needs a coach. It does not matter whether you are a basketball player, a tennis player, a gymnast or a bridge player.

Therefore, from honing skills and improving techniques to providing valuable guidance and support, mentors are indispensable assets that propel individuals towards achieving their goals and reaching their full potential. Mentors offer valuable insights, share their experiences, and provide guidance based on their successes and failures.

Mentors also serve as a source of inspiration and motivation. They instil confidence in their mentees and encourage them to pursue their goals and aspirations. Gates attributes much of his success to the mentors who inspired him to think big and strive for greatness.

Moreover, mentors provide valuable networks and connections. They open doors to opportunities and introduce mentees to influential individuals within their respective fields. Gates acknowledges the power of connections in achieving success and believes that mentors can be instrumental in helping individuals expand their networks and forge meaningful relationships.

However, Gates stresses that finding a mentor is not a one-size-fits-all approach. It requires proactive effort and a willingness to seek guidance. He encourages individuals to identify individuals who have succeeded in areas of interest and approach them with humility and a genuine desire to learn.

Furthermore, Gates believes in the importance of reciprocity in the mentor-mentee relationship. He highlights the value of mentees actively seeking to contribute and bring value to the mentorship dynamic. By sharing their unique perspectives and insights, mentees can offer fresh ideas and perspectives that can also benefit their mentors.

A mentor empowers us to see a possible future, even when everything seems Impossible, and believe it can be obtained. Thus, it is undeniable that everyone can benefit from having a mentor, as they serve as catalysts for improvement and facilitators of personal and professional growth.

Lesson: *Everyone needs a mentor in life for guidance, irrespective of the chosen career field.*

❑

Do Not Lament or Complaint About Miseries

Life is filled with ups and downs, challenges and setbacks. It is natural to face hardships and experience moments of sadness and frustration. However, dwelling on our miseries and lamenting about them only prolongs our suffering and hinders or impedes our ability to move forward. Instead, adopting a positive mindset and embracing a more constructive approach to dealing with difficulties is crucial.

Lamenting about miseries often leads to a cycle of negativity. When we continuously focus on our problems and setbacks, it becomes difficult to see any potential solutions or opportunities for growth. We become trapped in a mindset that perpetuates our misery, hindering our ability to find new paths and create positive change. Hence, rather than lamenting or complaining about your problems, focus on finding potential solutions to your problems.

Gates says, "If you are born poor, it is not your mistake. But if you die poor, it is your mistake." No one can indeed choose the circumstances they are born in, including poverty. But it is also true that we can change our circumstances with our choices today. If your situation is unacceptable, you must make your circumstances acceptable to your needs.

Rather than lamenting the existing difficulties, Gates encourages individuals to channel their energy into finding practical solutions. He believes that leveraging technology, expertise, and resources makes it possible to make significant progress and create a better future for everyone.

Furthermore, lamenting about miseries tends to narrow our perspective, making it challenging to see the positive aspects of life. Practising gratitude and adopting a more positive outlook can help us appreciate what we have and find joy in the present moment. By shifting our focus towards gratitude and the opportunities for growth, we can cultivate a more fulfilling and optimistic mindset.

In addition, Gates believes that lamenting or complaining about miseries often leaves us feeling powerless and victimised by circumstances. However, by taking ownership of our lives and focusing on what we can control, we regain a sense of empowerment. Instead of dwelling on miseries, we can channel our energy towards actions that bring positive change and personal growth.

Finally, consistently focusing on miseries can consume our valuable time and energy that could be better spent on finding solutions or making progress. Instead of dwelling on the past or feeling stuck in a negative mindset, it is more productive to channel our efforts towards identifying actionable steps, learning from mistakes, and moving forward.

Therefore, adopt a positive attitude to prevent yourself from dwelling on your life's miseries. Remember that if you focus on miseries, you will end up manifesting miseries only. Hence, instead focus on optimistic thoughts to attract positive results.

Lesson: *Stop lamenting about miseries if you do not want to manifest more miseries in your life.*

❑

Innovation is the Heart and Soul of a Business

Innovation is often considered the lifeblood of any successful business. It serves as the driving force behind growth, adaptability, and competitive advantage. By embracing innovation, companies can stay ahead of the curve, meet evolving customer demands, and explore new opportunities.

According to Bill Gates, at the heart of every business, innovation fuels creativity, pushing boundaries and challenging the status quo. It encourages employees to think outside the box, find novel solutions, and implement transformative ideas. By fostering or encouraging a culture of innovation, organisations can harness the collective intelligence and talents of their workforce to drive positive change.

Furthermore, innovation enables businesses to develop groundbreaking products and services, revolutionise existing processes, and explore untapped markets. It allows companies to anticipate market trends, identify customer pain points, and deliver solutions that meet or exceed expectations. By continuously innovating, businesses can stay relevant in a rapidly changing world, maintain their competitive edge, and build long-term success.

Moreover, innovation promotes efficiency and effectiveness within organisations. It encourages the adoption of new technologies, streamlined workflows, and improved methodologies. By embracing innovation, businesses can optimise their operations, reduce costs, and enhance productivity. This not only benefits the organisation itself but also improves the overall customer experience.

Gates believes that innovation is not limited to product development; it extends to all aspects of a business, including marketing strategies, customer engagement, and organisational structures. Embracing innovative approaches in these areas can lead to improved brand perception, increased customer loyalty, and greater employee satisfaction.

However, Gates warns that it is important to note that innovation requires a supportive environment and a mindset that embraces change. Businesses must be willing to take risks, learn from failures, and adapt quickly to evolving circumstances. They should encourage collaboration, provide resources for research and development, and foster and promote a culture that values creativity and experimentation.

As Gates says, "I believe innovation is the most powerful force for change in the world. People who are pessimistic about the future tend to extrapolate from the present in a straight line. But innovation fundamentally shifts the trajectory of development." He adds, "Innovation is often the hidden thing, because we can't put numbers to it. And yet it's the thing that defines the way we live, the things we'd like to have for everyone whether it's health or education."

Therefore, it is essential to remember that for every business to become successful, innovation is must. It is the key to a bright future. It is innovation that separates leaders from followers. Innovation is not just about bringing positive changes and creating opportunities but it is all about adding value to people's lives.

Lesson: *Innovation is the heart and soul of a business.*

❑

Be Humble at All Times

Being humble at all times is a valuable virtue that can positively influence our interactions, relationships, and overall character. It entails maintaining a modest and respectful attitude, regardless of our achievements, status, or circumstances. It is a quality that has been widely recognised and admired by many successful individuals, including Bill Gates.

Bill Gates believes that being humble is crucial for continuous growth and improvement. It involves acknowledging one's limitations, valuing the perspectives and expertise of others, and being open to learning from diverse sources. Gates understands that no individual possesses all the knowledge or skills needed to tackle complex problems and make significant advancements. By staying humble, he encourages a mindset that values collaboration, teamwork, and the willingness to seek guidance and insights from others.

Gates also recognises the importance of humility in leadership. He believes that leaders who remain humble are more likely to inspire and motivate their teams effectively. By acknowledging the contributions and achievements of others, leaders can foster a positive and inclusive work environment where every individual feels valued and empowered. Humble leaders prioritise the success of the team and organisation over personal recognition and ego, creating a culture of trust, respect, and innovation.

As Gates has aptly said, “Success is an awful teacher. It seduces smart people into thinking they can’t lose.” Hence, it is essential to be humble even after achieving success because you do not want to be deceived in the falsehood of your invincibility. Furthermore, Gates believes that humility is closely linked to empathy and the ability to understand the needs and challenges of others. By approaching situations with humility, individuals can better connect with people from diverse backgrounds and experiences. This understanding enables them to make informed decisions, develop meaningful solutions, and contribute to positive social change.

Despite his remarkable success, Bill Gates remains grounded and committed to giving back to society. Through the Bill and Melinda Gates Foundation, he has dedicated significant resources to addressing global challenges such as poverty, healthcare, and education. Gates’ humble approach has allowed him to connect with those in need and work collaboratively with partners and experts to make a meaningful impact.

Hence, remember to be humble at all times because circumstances could change in a blink of an eye. In addition, striving to be humble at all times is a valuable mindset that can bring numerous benefits to our personal and social lives. Remember, a tree that wants to touch the sky, must extend its roots into earth for more rise upwards, more it has to go downwards. So to rise in life, we must be down to earth. Likewise, in order to achieve great heights and success, we must establish a strong foundation and connection to reality.

By being aware of our own capabilities and acknowledging that we do not have all the answers, we become open to learning, growth, and collaboration. Therefore, by staying connected to reality, recognising our limitations, valuing others, and maintaining humility and gratitude, we establish a strong foundation for growth, success, and meaningful relationships.

Lesson: *Be humble at all times.*

❑

Surround Yourself with Successful and Smart People

To become successful in life, you must surround yourself with like-minded people who share your vision and convictions. Thus, successful people always surround themselves with other success-minded people who are also experts in their field. Being in the company of successful and smart people is vital because it is our company that helps us determine who we become. The kind of company you have, the kind of person you will become. Hence, it is essential for you to surround ourselves with the right kind of people who motivates you to achieve your vision or life's ultimate goal or objective.

Bill Gates, himself lays emphasis on the importance of surrounding yourself with successful and smart people because he believes that this practice can significantly impact personal and professional growth. According to him, the people you surround yourself with have a profound influence on your own development and achievements. Often in interviews and speeches he is found saying, "Surround yourself with people who challenge you, teach you, and push you to be your better self." Therefore, remember that the more you surround yourself with people of high potential and calibre, the greater will be your chance to become successful.

Gates believes that being in the company of accomplished individuals can be a source of inspiration and motivation. When you see others achieving great things, it can spark a desire within you to reach for similar heights. Their successes serve as a reminder of what is possible or feasible and can push you to set ambitious goals for yourself.

Additionally, Gates believes that surrounding yourself with smart bright people provides unique learning opportunities. Interacting with individuals who possess deep knowledge and expertise in various fields exposes you to new ideas and perspectives. Their insights and experiences can broaden your understanding and enable you to approach challenges in innovative ways.

Moreover, Gates highlights the importance of networking and building connections with successful individuals. By surrounding yourself with such individuals, you gain access to their networks, which can open doors to new opportunities and collaborations. These connections can be instrumental in advancing your own endeavours and expanding your reach.

Furthermore, Gates emphasises the significance of the positive influence that successful and smart people can have on your mindset and behaviour. Their discipline, work ethic, and problem-solving abilities can rub off on you, helping you develop similar traits and habits. Being around individuals who embody excellence can shape your own approach to work and life.

It is essential to remember that surrounding yourself with successful and smart people is not about comparison or competition. It is about creating an environment that fosters growth, learning, and mutual support. Embrace the opportunity to connect with such individuals and cultivate relationships that contribute positively to your own journey. Remember, you are the product of your environment, so surround yourself with the best.

Lesson: *Surround yourself with people who challenge you, teach you, and push or induce you to be your better self.*

❑

Do What You Love

When it comes to doing what you love, it is about more than just pursuing a hobby or engaging in enjoyable activities. It is about finding work or a career that aligns with your passions, interests, and values. When we do what we love, we start loving what we do. It will make putting extra efforts in your work easier, which in return push you towards success.

Bill Gates once said, "I think it is very important to do what you love and to follow your passion because if you do that, then things will work out for you." When you engage in activities that you are passionate about, you are naturally more motivated. Passion brings a sense of enthusiasm and energy, making it easier to overcome obstacles and persist through challenges. It fuels your drive to excel and pushes you to continually improve. Moreover, doing what you love can bring a deep sense of fulfilment and happiness. When you are engaged in work that resonates with your interests, you derive a genuine sense of satisfaction from your accomplishments. It provides a meaningful purpose and a sense of fulfilment that extends beyond financial rewards.

Gates also believes that when you love what you do, you are more likely to be productive and efficient. The tasks at hand do not feel like a burden, but rather as opportunities for personal growth and expression. This heightened productivity often leads to better results and success in your chosen field. Furthermore, pursuing your passions encourages a lifelong commitment to learning and personal development. When you are genuinely interested in a subject or field, you naturally seek out new knowledge, skills, and experiences related to it. This continuous learning enhances your expertise and keeps you at the forefront of your chosen domain.

Gates does recognise that doing what you love does not mean it will always be easy or devoid of challenges. However, your passion can help you overcome those challenges more effectively. Your love for the work gives you the resilience and determination to persevere in the face of obstacles. You are more likely to find innovative solutions and maintain a positive mindset during difficult times.

Besides when you are passionate about what you do, you have the opportunity to make a positive impact on others. Your enthusiasm and dedication can inspire and motivate those around you. Whether it is through creating innovative products, providing exceptional service, or contributing to meaningful causes, you have the potential to influence and uplift others.

As Steve Jobs once said, “Your work is going to fill a large part of your life, and the only way to be truly satisfied is to do what you believe is great work. And the only way to do great work is to love what you do. If you haven’t found it yet, keep looking. Don’t settle. As with all matters of the heart, you will know when you find it.” So, find a career or job that you like the best and while doing it get someone who will pay you for doing your job.

Lesson: *The most effective way to find success is to do what you love.*

❑

Make the Product Aesthetically Good Looking

Bill Gates has often emphasised the importance of making products visually appealing and well-designed. While he is primarily known for his expertise in technology and business, Gates recognises that aesthetics play a significant role in the success of a product. He understands while it is ideal to produce something of high quality, if that is not attainable, it is still essential to ensure it appears aesthetically pleasing to customers.

Gates understands that consumers are drawn to products that not only offer great functionality but also have an appealing design. He believes that a visually pleasing product can enhance the user experience and create a positive emotional connection with the consumer.

In his book *The Road Ahead*, written in collaboration with Nathan Myhrvold and Peter Rinearson, Gates wrote about the significance of design in the tech industry. He acknowledged that while functionality and performance are crucial, a product's aesthetics should not be overlooked. Gates stated, "It is more than just making a device that works. It is making a device that looks great and feels great to use."

Gates even once said, "If you can't make it good, at least make it look good." He acknowledges that creating something truly excellent, be it a product, service, or any other endeavour, is the ideal objective. However, in situations where achieving perfection is not possible or practical, he suggests that aesthetics can still play a significant role. In today's visually-oriented world, appearance often influences perception and initial impressions. People tend to gravitate towards visually appealing things, assuming they are of higher quality. By focusing on aesthetics, one can enhance the perception of value and create a positive first impression, even if the underlying substance is not flawless.

At the same time, Gates also highlighted the importance of simplicity in design. He advocated for products that are intuitive and easy to use, with a clean and elegant interface. Gates believes that simplicity enhances usability and allows users to engage with the product more effectively.

In recent years, Gates has become more involved in philanthropic efforts through the Bill and Melinda Gates

Foundation. However, his appreciation for good design and aesthetics remains evident. Gates recognises that even in the realm of social initiatives and global health, the visual appeal of campaigns and solutions can greatly influence their effectiveness.

Overall, Bill Gates understands that a product's design and aesthetics are essential elements in capturing consumer interest and satisfaction. By combining functionality, simplicity, and visual appeal, Gates believes that companies can create products that not only excel in performance but also delight users with their aesthetics. However, it is also crucial to maintain a balance between appearance and functionality of product, ensuring that the underlying quality meets or exceeds expectations.

Lesson: *To attract more customers make the product aesthetically good looking and inviting.*

❑

Competition Keeps You on Your Toes

Competition in business is important for several reasons, as it drives innovation, encourages efficiency, benefits consumers, and fosters overall economic growth. Bill Gates has consistently emphasised on the importance of healthy competition in driving innovation and progress. He believes that competition is a powerful force that keeps individuals and organisations on their toes, spurring them to constantly improve and strive for excellence.

In his book *The Road Ahead*, Gates discussed the role a healthy competition plays in business. Though he acknowledged that at times any competition can be intense, but it as a positive force that motivates companies to push the boundaries of what is possible. Gates wrote, "Competition is a rude yet effective motivator." He further continued, "Whether it's Google or Apple or free software, we have got some fantastic competitors and it keeps us on our toes."

Gates understands that when companies compete, they are driven to innovate and differentiate themselves from their rivals. The desire to stay ahead and gain a competitive edge fuels the development of new ideas, technologies, and products. This ultimately benefits consumers by offering them a wider range of options and driving advancements in various fields.

Moreover, Gates believes that competition encourages continuous improvement. When organisations are in a competitive environment, they are constantly challenged to find better ways of doing things, enhancing their products or services, and meeting customer demands more effectively. Gates once said, "Your most unhappy customers are your greatest source of learning." It is crucial to remember that without competition, there is a risk of complacency and companies may lose their touch with the evolving demands of the market.

Throughout his career, Gates has witnessed the power of healthy competition firsthand. Microsoft's success and impact on the technology industry were partly due to its ability to compete and adapt to changing market conditions. Gates understood that complacency and resting on past achievements would hinder or hamper progress, and he encouraged his employees to embrace competition as a means of driving innovation.

Furthermore, competitors provide valuable learning opportunities through their successes and failures. By observing and analysing their strategies, companies can gain insights that shape their own approaches and aid in making informed decisions. This learning process enables companies to stay and remained ahead in the competitive landscape, fostering innovation, differentiation, and the provision of unique value to customers.

Overall, a healthy competition is a catalyst for progress and innovation. It as a driving force that pushes individuals and organisations to constantly improve and find better ways of doing things. It creates a dynamic ecosystem where companies are driven to deliver exceptional products and services to meet customer expectations and demands. This relentless pursuit of excellence ultimately benefits customers, as they are presented with a wider range of innovative choices and improved experiences. Hence, a healthy competition is crucial for success to push us constantly towards improvement.

Lesson: *Competition is a rude yet effective motivator. It keeps you on your toes.*

❑

Business and Technology Go Together

Technology plays a pivotal role in driving the success and growth of businesses. This is why, Bill Gates strongly believes that business and technology are interconnected and go hand in hand. Throughout his career, he has consistently emphasised on the crucial role that technology plays in driving business innovation, growth, and success. In fact, Gates once said, "The first rule of any technology used in a business is that automation applied to an efficient operation will magnify the efficiency. The second is that automation applied to an inefficient operation will magnify the inefficiency."

Gates understands that in today's digital age, technology enables businesses to streamline their operations, automate processes, and improve overall efficiency. From utilising software systems for inventory management to implementing customer relationship management (CRM) tools for sales and marketing, businesses rely on technology to optimise their internal processes and reduce costs.

According to Gates, technology facilitates seamless communication and collaboration within businesses. It also enables businesses to engage with customers and partners through various digital platforms, enhancing communication and fostering collaboration across different stakeholders.

Moreover, in today's data-driven world, businesses require to gather vast amounts of information. Technology provides the tools and infrastructure to collect, store, manage, and analyze this data effectively. Businesses leverage data analytics and business intelligence tools to gain insights, make informed decisions, and identify opportunities for growth and improvement.

Similarly, technology has also revolutionised how businesses interact with customers and reach their target markets. Websites, e-commerce platforms, and social media channels allow businesses to expand their market reach, engage with customers directly, and gather valuable feedback. Technology also enables personalised marketing campaigns, customer relationship management, and targeted advertising, enhancing customer experiences and driving business growth.

Furthermore, Gates believes that technology is a catalyst for innovation, driving businesses to develop new products, services, and business models. Adopting emerging technologies such as artificial intelligence, machine learning, Internet of Things (IoT), and blockchain can provide businesses with a competitive advantage. Technology also empowers businesses to disrupt traditional industries, create unique value propositions, and differentiate themselves in the market.

Hence, it is right to believe that business and technology are inseparable. Technology is not only a tool but a strategic imperative for businesses. All told, it empowers businesses by enhancing operational efficiency, enabling effective communication and collaboration, facilitating data-driven decision-making, expanding market reach, fostering innovation, and managing risks. This is why, Gates encourages businesses to embrace technology, leverage its potential, and stay at the forefront of innovation to drive growth, improve efficiency, and make a positive impact on society.

Lesson: *Business and technology are inextricably interwoven. No one can talk meaningfully about one without talking about the other.*

❑

Never Stop Learning

Never stop learning is a mantra that emphasises the importance of continual personal growth and the pursuit of knowledge throughout one's life. It encourages individuals to adopt a mindset of curiosity, exploration, and self-improvement. According to Gates, learning is not limited to formal education or academic institutions. He believes that learning should be a lifelong journey, driven by curiosity and a thirst for knowledge. Gates encourages individuals to seek knowledge in various forms, whether through reading books, attending lectures, engaging in meaningful conversations, or exploring new experiences. He recommends an open mind and a willingness to embrace new ideas and perspectives.

Gates recognises that the world is constantly changing, and new information is being generated at an unprecedented rate. To stay relevant and adapt to these changes, he asserts that continuous learning is crucial. He emphasises that individuals who embrace lifelong learning are better equipped to face the challenges and opportunities of the future. By constantly expanding their knowledge and skills, they can remain adaptable, innovative, and successful in an rapidly-evolving world.

Furthermore, Gates believes that learning should be driven by passion and personal interests. He encourages people to pursue subjects that genuinely intrigue them, as this intrinsic motivation fosters a deeper and more meaningful understanding. Gates himself is an avid reader, known for devouring books on a wide range of topics. He credits his voracious reading habit for broadening his perspectives and inspiring his ideas and innovations.

Gates acknowledges that learning can sometimes be challenging and requires effort and dedication. However, he believes that the rewards of lifelong learning are immeasurable. It not only enriches individuals' lives but also contributes to their personal and professional success. Moreover, never stop learning fosters intellectual curiosity and a thirst for knowledge. It encourages individuals to explore diverse topics, disciplines, and perspectives, broadening their understanding of the world. Through reading books, attending seminars, engaging in discussions, or even experimenting with new hobbies, people can discover new interests and expand their horizons.

Additionally, never stop learning nurtures critical thinking and problem-solving abilities. By consistently seeking new information and engaging in analytical thought processes, individuals can sharpen their cognitive skills and enhance their ability to tackle complex challenges. This capacity for critical thinking becomes particularly valuable in a rapidly changing and interconnected world, where new problems and opportunities constantly arise.

Moreover, continuous learning contributes to personal fulfilment and self-actualization. It provides a sense of accomplishment, as individuals acquire new knowledge and master new skills. Learning can also foster personal growth by helping individuals gain a deeper understanding of themselves, their passions, and their values. It enables individuals to set and achieve meaningful goals, leading to a sense of purpose and fulfilment in life.

Never stop learning also promotes adaptability and resilience. In today's fast-paced world, where technological advancements and societal shifts occur at a rapid pace, those who embrace lifelong learning are better equipped to navigate change. By constantly updating their knowledge and skills, individuals can remain agile, seize new opportunities, and overcome obstacles more effectively.

As Gates says, "You do not really start getting old till you stop learning, every book teaches me something new or helps me see things differently." Hence, the journey of learning is not merely about accumulating information but about embracing a mindset of growth and the endless possibilities it brings.

Lesson: *Never stop learning.*

❑

Do Not Let Complexity Stop You

Bill Gates has often shared insights on the importance of not allowing complexity to hinder progress and innovation. He believes that tackling complex challenges is essential for driving positive change and achieving ambitious goals. Gates encourages individuals and organisations to embrace complexity, break it down into manageable parts, and persevere in the face of daunting obstacles.

Gates recognises that complex problems often arise in various domains, including technology, business, and social issues. Rather than being discouraged by the intricacies involved, he urges individuals to approach complexity with determination and a problem-solving mindset. Gates believes that complex challenges present opportunities for innovation and discovery.

To overcome complexity, Gates stresses the importance of breaking problems down into smaller, more manageable components. By dissecting complex issues, individuals can focus on specific aspects, analyse them thoroughly, and develop targeted solutions. This approach allows for a more systematic and effective problem-solving process, making complexity more approachable and solvable.

Gates also stresses the value of collaboration and the power of diverse perspectives in tackling complex challenges. He believes that by bringing together individuals with different backgrounds, expertise, and experiences, teams can better understand the complexity at hand and devise innovative solutions. By fostering an environment that encourages collaboration, Gates encourages individuals to leverage collective intelligence to overcome complexity.

Furthermore, Gates highlights the significance of perseverance and resilience in the face of complex problems. He acknowledges that addressing intricate issues requires time, effort, and an unwavering commitment. Gates encourages individuals not to be discouraged by setbacks or initial failures but to view them as learning opportunities. By remaining persistent, adaptable, and willing to iterate, individuals can navigate the complexities and ultimately find successful solutions.

Gates also emphasises the need for continuous learning when facing complexity. He believes that staying informed, curious, and open-minded is crucial in understanding complex systems and developing effective strategies. Gates encourages individuals to constantly seek new knowledge, stay updated on advancements, and leverage insights from various fields to address complex challenges.

In a speech, while addressing students, Gates observed, "In line with this promise of this age, I want to exhort each of the graduates here to take on an issue, a complex problem, a deep inequity and become a specialist on it. if you make it the focus of your career, that would be phenomenal." He continued, "But you do not have to do that to make an impact. For the few hours of every week, you can use the growing power of the internet to get informed, find others with same interest, see the barriers and find ways to cut through them. Do not let complexity stop. Be activists. Take on big inequities. I feel sure, it would be one of the great experiences of your lives."

Therefore, take inspiration from Gates' advice and do not let any kind of complexity stop you from achieving your goals. Take down the greatest challenge as the greatest opportunity to show the world that you are here in this world to bring impactful changes and not to just exist without making a meaningful contribution to the society.

Lesson: *Tackling complex challenges is essential for driving positive change and achieving ambitious goals.*

❑

Elevate Humanity with Acts of Compassion

Bill Gates has consistently emphasised the importance of helping others and the need to act without waiting to become wealthy. Gates believes that making a positive impact and contributing to the well-being of others should be a fundamental aspect of everyone's life, regardless of their financial status.

According to Gates, helping others is not solely the responsibility of those who have amassed enormous wealth. He firmly believes that anyone, regardless of their financial means, has the capacity to make a positive impact in the lives of others. Gates advocates for the idea that kindness and compassion are not limited to material possessions but can be expressed through simple acts of empathy, support, and understanding.

Gates encourages individuals to act on their desire to help others from an early stage, without waiting to accumulate significant wealth. He believes that making a difference can start with small, meaningful gestures that have a profound impact. Whether it is volunteering time, sharing knowledge, or offering a helping hand to someone in need, Gates stresses the importance of taking action and cultivating a mindset of giving from the outset.

To emphasise the importance of acts of compassion, Gates recounted an incident from his early days, when he was neither rich nor famous. While at the New York airport, Gates wanted to buy a newspaper but realised he did not have enough change. He returned it to the vendor, explaining his lack of change. Surprisingly, the vendor insisted on giving it to him for free. Months later, in a similar situation, the vendor offered another newspaper, which Gates initially declined. The vendor assured him that he was sharing from his profit. After becoming wealthy and famous, Gates sought out the vendor to repay his kindness. However, the vendor humbly stated that Gates could never match his help, as he gave when he was poor. Gates realised that true wealth lies in a rich heart, not money, and kindness makes one beautiful, regardless of possessions.

Furthermore, Gates emphasises that the act of helping others is not only beneficial to the recipients but also personally rewarding and fulfilling. He believes that the satisfaction derived from making a positive impact is invaluable, regardless of one's financial status. Gates highlights the joy and sense of purpose that comes from improving the lives of others and contributing to the greater good and well-being of society.

Gates' own philanthropic endeavours exemplify his commitment to helping others. Through the Bill and Melinda Gates Foundation, he has dedicated substantial resources and efforts to address global challenges such as poverty, healthcare, and education. However, Gates also acknowledges that philanthropy is not limited to large-scale initiatives and that even individual actions can create a ripple effect of positive change.

Therefore, always remember that wealth is not merely about money but also about having a rich heart filled with kindness and compassion. Acts of kindness and compassion are necessary because without them humanity cannot survive. So, help others as much as you can and any way you can.

Lesson: *Acts of kindness and compassion help to elevate humanity.*

❑

Television is Not Real Life

Bill Gates has often expressed his view that television does not accurately represent real life. He believes that while television can be entertaining and informative, it often fails to provide a realistic portrayal of the world we live in. Gates emphasises the need for individuals to recognise the distinction between television and the actual complexities and nuances of everyday life.

According to Gates, television shows and movies are designed for entertainment purposes and are crafted to capture attention and engage audiences. However, they are not meant to be a reflection of reality. The storylines, characters, and situations depicted on screen are often dramatised, simplified, or exaggerated for dramatic effect, which can create distorted perceptions and unrealistic expectations.

Gates once said, "Television is not real life. In real life, people actually have to leave the coffee shops and go to jobs." Here in the context of the coffee shop analogy, the message conveys that in real life, people have responsibilities and obligations that extend beyond the leisurely atmosphere of a coffee shop. While television shows may frequently depict characters spending prolonged periods in coffee shops, engaging in leisurely activities and socialising without any mention of work, this is not reflective of the typical routines of most individuals.

Real life involves a variety of commitments, such as employment, education, family responsibilities, and personal pursuits, that necessitate leaving the coffee shop and actively participating in different aspects of life. People have jobs and careers that require their attention and engagement. They have deadlines, tasks, and responsibilities that need to be fulfilled to support themselves and contribute to society.

Therefore, it is essential for individuals to remember that the ideal life they visualise after being inspired from fictionalised portrayals is far different from the actual demands of life. By doing so, people can avoid falling into the trap of comparing their own experiences to the idealized versions shown on TV, which can lead to unrealistic expectations or feelings of inadequacy.

Moreover, understanding that television serves as a form of entertainment and storytelling helps individuals prioritise their time and energy. It reminds them to focus on real-world responsibilities, such as pursuing careers, honing skills, and contributing meaningfully to society. By acknowledging the limitations of television in representing the full spectrum of human experiences, individuals can make informed decisions and set realistic expectations for themselves.

In essence, Gates urges individuals to embrace the complexities and obligations of real life, leaving behind the fictionalised narratives that may perpetuate misconceptions or unrealistic ideals.

> **Lesson:** *Television is not real life. There is more going on behind the scenes where you have to focus on real-world responsibilities.*

❑

Make Your Own Path

Bill Gates has often stressed the importance of making your own path in life. He believes that following the conventional or prescribed routes may limit one's potential for growth and success. Gates encourages individuals to think independently, take risks, and chart their own course.

According to Gates, making your own path involves being proactive and carving out your unique journey, rather than simply following the well-trodden paths that others have taken. To create your own path means to forge a unique and personalised journey through life that aligns with your aspirations, values, and passions. It requires thinking critically, questioning the status quo, and seeking innovative solutions to problems. Gates himself is a prime example of someone who defied traditional paths and built his own extraordinary success story by co-founding Microsoft and revolutionising the technology industry.

Gates believes that embracing entrepreneurship, creativity, and a willingness to take risks are vital components of making your own path. He encourages individuals to pursue their passions, explore their interests, and not be afraid to deviate from societal expectations or norms. Gates recognises that forging a new path can be challenging, but he believes that the rewards are often worth the effort.

According to Gates, creating your own path is important for several reasons. Firstly, it enables you to live a life of authenticity. By aligning your actions with your values and passions, you can experience a sense of congruence and fulfilment. It allows you to make choices that resonate with your true self, leading to greater satisfaction and happiness.

Secondly, creating your own path allows you to unleash your creativity and innovation. By thinking independently and challenging conventional wisdom, you can break new ground and find unique solutions to problems. It opens up opportunities for personal growth, self-expression, and making a positive impact in your chosen field or community.

Moreover, creating your own path promotes self-reliance and personal empowerment. It encourages you to assume ownership of your decisions and actions, rather than relying on others to determine your path. It fosters a sense of responsibility and accountability, empowering you to overcome obstacles, learn from failures, and adapt to changing circumstances.

Creating your own path also cultivates resilience and a growth mindset. It requires embracing uncertainty, taking calculated risks, and learning from setbacks. By stepping outside your comfort zone and facing challenges head-on, you develop valuable skills, expand your capabilities, and build the confidence to navigate future endeavours.

Finally, creating your own path allows you to leave a lasting legacy. By following your passions and pursuing meaningful goals, you can make a unique contribution to the world. Enabling you to make a positive difference, inspire others, and leave behind a footprint that reflects your values and accomplishments.

So, remember that you do not have to live a life that others define for you because it is acceptable, live a life that others do not understand. They do not need to because it is not their life. We are the only one responsible ones the choices we make in our life so we do not have to defend our choices. So, create your own legacy.

Lesson: *Make your own path because you do not have to be like others.*

❑

Focus on One Thing at a Time

Bill Gates has emphasised the importance of focusing on one thing at a time in order to achieve success. He believes that multitasking and spreading one's attention too thin can obstruct or hamper productivity and hinder the ability to make significant progress.

In an interview, Gates once said, "My success, part of it certainly, is that I have focused on a few selective things." He continued, "Only through focus can you do world-class things, no matter how capable you are." According to Gates, focusing on one thing at a time is important for several reasons and it plays a crucial role in achieving success.

Firstly, when you focus on one thing at a time, you can allocate your full attention and energy to that task or goal. This deep level of concentration allows you to work more efficiently and productively, leading to higher-quality output and better results.

Secondly, by focusing on one thing, you can dedicate more time and mental resources to understanding and analysing the details and complexities involved. This enables you to make better-informed decisions, consider various perspectives, and evaluate potential outcomes more thoroughly.

Moreover, it allows you to develop a higher level of expertise and mastery in that particular area. By devoting concentrated effort and practice, you can refine your skills, gain in-depth knowledge, and become more proficient, making you more effective and influential in your chosen field.

In addition, multitasking can lead to divided attention and increased chances of errors. By focusing on one task at a time, you can minimize distractions, maintain a clear mind, and reduce the likelihood of mistakes or oversights. This attention to detail enhances the quality and accuracy of your work.

Furthermore, immersing yourself in one task or project allows you to explore it more deeply. By delving into the intricacies and nuances, you gain a comprehensive understanding that can spark creative ideas and innovative solutions. This depth of understanding fosters originality and pushes boundaries, propelling you towards success.

Focusing on one thing also enables you to make consistent progress towards your goals. By channelling your efforts into a singular objective, you can stay on track, overcome challenges more effectively, and make steady advancements. This progress builds momentum and propels you closer to achieving your desired outcomes.

Finally, focusing on one thing helps you manage your time more efficiently. By prioritising and dedicating specific blocks of time to individual tasks, you can create a structured schedule that optimises productivity and minimises time wastage. This disciplined approach maximizes your output and allows you to accomplish more in less time.

In conclusion, to be successful in all your endeavours, you must focus on one thing at a time. Concentrating on one thing without interruption is the best way to get meaningful work done. This is the only way to become productive and advance in this world.

Lesson: *Focus on one thing at a time because spreading one's attention too thin can hinder or impede productivity.*

❑

Work Hard and No Excuses

Bill Gates has long emphasised the value of working hard without making excuses as a key ingredient for success. He firmly believes that achieving significant accomplishments requires unwavering dedication, relentless effort, and a refusal to let obstacles obstruct progress.

According to Gates, working hard without excuses means taking full responsibility for one's actions and outcomes. It entails acknowledging that success is not handed on a silver platter but is earned through perseverance and a strong work ethic. Gates himself is known for his relentless pursuit of excellence and his willingness to take ownership of his endeavours.

Gates believes that working hard pushes you outside your comfort zone and helps you develop new skills, expand your knowledge, and enhance your abilities. It challenges you to overcome obstacles, learn from failures, and continually improve, leading to personal growth and development.

Moreover, success often requires persistent effort and dedication. By working hard without making excuses, you stay focused on your goals and increase your chances of achieving them. It helps you stay motivated, maintain momentum, and make consistent progress towards your desired outcomes.

Furthermore, working hard without excuses cultivates discipline and a sense of responsibility. It instils a strong work ethic, teaching you the value of perseverance, commitment, and taking ownership of your actions. This discipline and responsibility are essential qualities for achieving long-term success.

Recalling his 20s, Gates in an interview once said, “I think your habits are sort of set in your 20s and 30s. By my standards in the 20s, I didn’t believe in weekends back then, not to mention in vacations.” He continued, “In my 20s, I was a true fanatic. I believed in working on software night and day.” These statements show his dedication towards his goal and work. This is why Gates advises individuals to work hard without making any excuses like fatigue, sickness, holidays, etc. For he believes that if you are truly passionate about your dream or vision, you will work consistently irrespective of the circumstances.

Gates also believes that perseverance helps you confront and overcome challenges and setbacks. Instead of making excuses, you should approach difficulties with determination and resilience. This mindset enables you to find creative solutions, adapt to changing circumstances, and persevere in the face of adversity.

In addition, when you consistently work hard without making excuses, you earn the respect and admiration of others. People appreciate individuals who show dedication, reliability, and a willingness to go the extra mile. Diligence helps you build a reputation as someone who can be relied upon and trusted, opening doors to new opportunities and collaborations.

Finally, by working hard without making excuses, you inspire and motivate others around you. Your dedication and perseverance serve as a role model for colleagues, friends, and family members, encouraging them to adopt a similar work ethic and strive for their own success. Therefore, you should work hard and stay committed to your aspirations so that you could increase your chances of reaching new heights of achievement and fulfilment.

Lesson: *To achieve success, work hard consistently irrespective of the circumstances. Making excuses will not help you in the long run.*

❑

Start Measuring Yourself

Bill Gates has always emphasised the importance of measuring oneself as a key aspect of personal and professional growth. He believes that by measuring our progress and performance, we can gain valuable insights and make informed decisions to drive improvement and achieve success.

According to Gates, measurement allows us to understand where we stand in relation to our goals and aspirations. It provides a benchmark to assess our current abilities and progress. By setting specific metrics and tracking our performance, we can objectively evaluate our strengths, weaknesses, and areas for improvement.

Gates suggests that measuring oneself fosters a mindset of continuous learning and improvement. It enables us to identify patterns, trends, and areas of inefficiency, empowering us to make necessary adjustments and optimise our efforts. By measuring our performance, we can set specific targets, track our progress, and make data-driven decisions to enhance our effectiveness.

Gates once said, "I think the ability that has helped in many things is a kind of measurement scientific framework, where I go in say, 'Did anybody handle this well? What are the best practices? Do we have numbers on that?'" He further said, "Let's get everybody measuring what they are doing so that they can strive to match what that the best measurement is for us is often. So, for me I always looked at how we do measure better measurement and use that drive the very best practices."

Basically, Gates believes that measurement promotes accountability. When we have clear metrics and targets, we hold ourselves accountable for our actions and outcomes. It encourages us to take responsibility and strive for excellence in our endeavours. Gates often emphasises the importance of taking ownership and holding ourselves to high standards to drive meaningful progress.

Gates also emphasises the power of feedback in the measurement process. Seeking feedback from others, whether through mentors, peers, or customers, can provide valuable insights into our strengths and areas for development. Incorporating feedback into our self-measurement allows us to gain different perspectives and make necessary adjustments to enhance our performance.

Thus, Bill Gates encourages individuals to start measuring themselves as a means of personal and professional growth. By setting clear metrics, tracking progress, and seeking feedback, we can gain valuable insights, make informed decisions, and continuously improve. Measurement fosters accountability, promotes a growth mindset, and enables us to optimize our efforts to achieve success. Gates believes that by measuring ourselves, we can unlock our full potential and make meaningful contributions in our chosen endeavours.

Lesson: *Start measuring yourself because it helps you to monitor your rate of progress towards your goal or objective.*

❑

Do Not Procrastinate

Procrastination means delaying or postponing tasks or actions that need to be completed. It involves putting off important activities in favour of more immediate and often less significant ones. While everyone may experience bouts of procrastination from time to time, it is generally considered an undesirable habit due to its negative impact on productivity and overall well-being.

According to Gates, procrastination is detrimental for success. It creates hindrance to success and productivity. It prevents individuals from achieving their goals and reaching their full potential. Gates believes that by procrastinating, we waste valuable time and opportunities that could have been utilised more effectively.

Moreover, procrastination often leads to increased stress and anxiety. The looming deadlines and the constant reminder of unfinished tasks can create a sense of pressure and overwhelm. By tackling tasks in a timely manner, we can reduce stress levels and maintain a healthier work-life balance.

Furthermore, Gates believes that procrastination can result in missed opportunities. When we postpone important tasks, we may miss deadlines, lose out on potential collaborations or promotions, and hinder personal growth. By taking prompt action, we can seize opportunities as they arise and make the most of them.

Also, the act of procrastinating can negatively impact our motivation and enthusiasm for completing tasks. As we delay, we may experience a lack of momentum and find it increasingly difficult to regain focus and motivation. By avoiding procrastination, we can maintain a steady flow of motivation and stay engaged in our work.

In an interview, recalling his college days Gates said, "When I was in college, I developed a bad habit where I used to show people that I did not do any work and I didn't go to classes and I didn't care. At the very last minute, like two days before the test I would get serious about it and people thought that was funny." He continued, "When I went into business that was a really bad habit and it took me a few years to get over that. Nobody praised because I would do things at the last minute and I tried to reverse that. Basically, procrastination is not a good habit." Therefore, one should avoid procrastination if they want to achieve success.

Gates also reminds that consistent procrastination can damage our reputation, both personally and professionally. Others may view us as unreliable or lacking commitment when we consistently delay tasks or miss deadlines. By demonstrating discipline and a proactive approach to tasks, we can build trust and credibility with others.

Finally, overcoming procrastination can contribute to personal growth. By practising self-discipline and effective time management, we develop valuable skills such as prioritisation, organisation, and perseverance. These skills not only enhance our productivity but also support our personal development and success.

Therefore, Gates believes that by avoiding procrastination, individuals can unlock their full potential and drive meaningful progress in their personal and professional lives.

Lesson: *Procrastination is a very bad and negative habit to have if you want to be successful.*

❑